Unforgivable
Seasons

Unforgivable Seasons

SHORT STORIES

Lady...?...

I get excited just the mere fact that we befriended one another & that we shared a wonderful class in something we enjoy doing. Thank you for your being Talking.

L. A. Davis

Diamonds & Pens in the Rough Publishing
Atlanta

Diamonds & Pens is my LLC — 2018 here I come!! :)

genuine — being you!! I love you to pieces!! I really mean this — Enjoy this Book — answer to pray for me as I do the same for you!!

(signature)

ISBN: 0692910557
ISBN 13: 9780692910559
Library of Congress Control Number: 2017909741
Diamonds & Pens, Ellenwood, GA

For my husband, Anthony, and my two amazing children,
Brea and Brandon:
I love you from the top to the bottom of my heart.

To everything there is a season, a time to every
activity under heaven. A time to be born and a
time to die.
A time to plant and a time to harvest.
A time to kill and a time to heal, time to build up.
A time to cry and a time to laugh.
A time to grieve and a time to dance.
A time to scatter stones and a time to gather stones.
A time to embrace and a time to turn away.
A time to search and a time to quit searching.
A time to keep and a time to throw away.
A time to tear and a time to mend.
A time to be quiet and a time to speak.
A time to love and a time to hate.
A time for war and a time for peace.

~Ecclesiastes 3:1–8

~Winter~

You are gonna catch a cold from the ice inside your soul.

~UNKNOWN

In Sickness, Health...Till Death

Tonight, I decided that this will be the last night I write in this journal. It's useless. Dumb. Ineffective. What's done is done. I have no more in me. I've always been told that I love hard and love the wrong ones. However, loving Robert has been different. My love for him feels like puppy love, always fresh and new. I know that marriages don't always maintain their fervor. People often tell me that you have to fight for love sometimes, and you must have lots of patience.

Robert and I were in our tenth year. We decided to wait for kids until he opened his law firm. He'd grown tired of waiting to become partner at his old firm, and he was ready to move on. I've always supported Robert in anything that he wants because this man has taken very good care of me. He satisfied me to the utmost—until he got that office. That's when he began to forget anniversaries, birthdays—you name it. We fought about everything. My looks. His looks. The coffee is too bitter. Toast is too hard. From too much of anything to not enough of everything. I always forgave him, but he would do it again and again. I knew that he was just "occupied" with his work and, of course, his clients. But he surprised me one night and decided to come home early.

"Hey, babe," I said, greeting him at the door. "You made it home early. Is everything OK?" Robert had started growing a beard. I didn't like it. I've always loved my Robert with a clean face. Somehow, we found ways to argue about this too.

"Yeah, yeah. Sure, it is. I know I've been putting in a lot of hours, and I felt the need to give my queen some much-needed attention." Robert turned and bent over to pick something up—a shopping bag from one of my favorite boutiques. "Here," he said. "I hope you like it. Let's shower and head out for dinner. Are you cool with that?"

I hesitated, pressing the dress against me. I had put on a few pounds, but tonight, this dress was going to be worn. "Yes, honey. Aw, you are indeed the sweetest. I appreciate this, and yes, I love it! Give me a few. I should be ready within an hour."

Robert grabbed my hand. "Sweetheart, don't take too long."

I smiled and winked at him and darted for the stairs.

The warmth of the water hit my body just right. I gleamed with every stroke of soap and water. He always knew how to make up and continue to be the man I married. I closed my eyes and turned toward the shower head, and there he was. My man. My husband. Robert joined me in the shower, warming my heart over and over again.

He gently kissed my neck, taking the sponge and lathering my body, which yearned for him. I turned to him, and we kissed long, hard, and passionately. He pressed his body against mine as he played with me and then entered me. I moaned so loudly that I was almost embarrassed. But the more I moaned, the more Robert gave it to me. The water ran so long that it became cold, but our bodies were hot and filled with passion. My hair was wet, and my legs were weak from multiple orgasms. We exited the shower and took turns drying each other.

As I took the towel to dry his back, I kissed him, feeling dazed. "Honey, we can stay in. I can whip up something or—"

Robert turned toward me. "I tell you what," he said. "Let's Uber a meal and some dessert. I'll place an order, and we can continue where we left off. You get dressed, and I'll set it up."

I bit my bottom lip and lightly swayed back and forth like a schoolgirl. "OK, do your thang, then. I'll be downstairs."

Robert walked over to the linen closet, grabbed a blanket, lit the fireplace, and then hit the remote for some music. The only outfit that would be appropriate for this event was something lacy or sheer. But why bother putting clothes on? A sheer thong and nothing else would top the night off.

That night, we barely ate any of the food that he ordered. We had our bubbly and made love for hours. It was a night that I will never forget. It was like the first time I met Robert. He was my first. He taught me everything. I was fresh out of high school, and we dated through college. We were friends before we exchanged vows. He was a man I've honored and cherished and trusted with every breath in me.

The next morning, I made us breakfast. I smiled at Robert as I sipped my cup of coffee and he read the paper. I felt like a million bucks. We both sat silently for a while, and then the conversation began.

"Monique, the next few months are going to be tight between us," he said. "I am telling you in advance that building this firm is not going to be easy for me. So, in the meantime, you need to find you something to do. You know, something to occupy your time. Maybe consider going back for your master's and becoming something more than a schoolteacher. While I am working, you, my dear, can study without any interruptions from me."

Robert's words were starting to irritate me. He made it sound as if he was not going to be around anymore—or much less often than he was already. And to plan what *he* thought was best for me almost pissed me off.

"So, Robert, sweetheart, you sound as if you have no plans to return home." I started laughing. "If I didn't know any better, that's what I'd think."

Robert peered over the newspaper. "Oh, Monique, don't start. We've been talking about me starting this firm for the longest. So don't start a fight now. The only thing I did not tell you is that I plan to stay at the corporate apartment instead of driving home every night."

I stood up, walked over to him, and pushed the paper down to the table. "Look," I said. "One, stop talking to me with the paper in front of you like that. I deserve more respect than that. And two, we never, *never* discussed an apartment anywhere. I mean, Robert, if we do this, we might as well..."

Robert stood up and looked down at me. "Do what, Monique? Break up? Separate? Do what? I've been supporting both of us for years now. And this living arrangement is only a temporary situation."

All sorts of thoughts raced through my mind, including thoughts of slapping the living crap out of him. The nerve of him, standing up to me indignantly and saying those words, any words concerning our vows. We've always said that we would never break our vows. We were for each other no matter what. Now this. An apartment. My returning to school after he didn't want me to go to school. And the freaking audacity to even think or say anything about a split. I walked away from Robert and put the breakfast dishes away. At this point, our conversation was over. I began to walk toward the stairs. "Robert, if you ever speak to me or make decisions like this again, we are going to have some serious problems. Have a nice day at work, honey."

I enrolled at Central University, thinking it would be good to attend classes on campus rather than online. It would break up the loneliness I was about to endure. I still could not stop thinking about the conversation we had last week. It was obvious that Robert was looking out for only himself. Since that last conversation, we had not spoken much. I had never been so angry with him.

Today, I would try to reach out to him. He had already moved to an apartment and told me that I could come over anytime. Unfortunately, I had no desire to stop by to see Robert. It seemed that lately, he had a different agenda. For years, I'd put off the things that were important to me—me as a teacher. Robert talked about that as if it was a bad place to be. He often said that teaching at that school, being around those kids, would only keep my mind in a fog; that being a teacher was the greatest influence on my desire to be a mother. I am not sure why Robert was so against being a parent. My body longed to have babies. After all, isn't that the number one desire and hope? To become a mother? The bottom line is that I did not like the fact that he felt that he could make decisions and move forward without at least giving me any notice or say in the matter.

I knew that any other woman would think that Robert was hiding another family or that he wanted this apartment so he'd have a place to cheat—especially because he wanted me to be busy. He wanted me out of his hair. However, I know my Robert, and these negative ideas were the furthest thing from his mind. He was not that type of man. He only had me at heart—he only wanted the best for me. But lately, it appeared that the best was only for him.

I decided to take the tour with the rest of the group that had assembled for the open house. The campus was not as big as I thought it would be. Besides, the majority of my courses would be in the humanities building. As I walked through the halls, a new thought came to mind. Instead of working toward my master's degree to help me as a teacher, perhaps it wouldn't be a bad idea to become a professor. But what would be my area of interest be? I had to think about it. "This campus seems to have a lot of extracurricular activities with the career and working adult in mind," I mumbled to myself.

A tall man turned around and said, "Excuse me, ma'am. Did you have a question?"

I was embarrassed for talking aloud and did not realize that anyone had heard me. "No, no. I was just admiring the building and the fact that there are things other than just classes for students to engage in."

The man passed me his card. "My name is Professor Billingsley. Monroe Billingsley. I am the director of the humanities department, and I also teach a few classes twice a week."

I moved my folder to my left hand and extended my right hand for a handshake. "Oh, wow…I mean, I'm pleased to meet you. My name is Monique Sails. I am returning to pursue my master's in…" I laughed. "Well, I have not quite decided yet." How embarrassing again, I thought.

"It's OK if you're not ready to commit to an exact concentration," he said. "But at least you have an idea. Welcome, and I hope to see you around soon. Be sure to use my card for any questions that you may have. Have an awesome day, Miss…"

I quickly corrected him. "Mrs. It's Mrs. Sails, and thank you. I will keep your card handy. I don't think that I'll have the need to bother you, but I will keep the card handy, Professor Billingsley. You have a great day as well."

My phone started buzzing in my purse. I opened the case, and it was Robert.

"Hey, honey. How is it going? We need to talk. Are you available for lunch?"

I arrived at Cashews Bar and Grille before Robert did. I decided to sit at the bar and have an appetizer and a glass of Pinot Noir. Robert was typically a little late, but because this lunch date had sounded urgent, I hoped that he would not be too late today. It had been a week since we'd really talked to each other. It hurt to be in this space with the person I was in love with.

I glanced at my watch, and it was 2:15 p.m. Robert had asked if we could meet at 1:30 p.m. I called him, and there was no answer. I sent a text. No answer. I ordered another glass of wine. The wine helped me to be less anxious during the wait. I kept peering at the door to see if he was about to walk into the restaurant. No Robert. I hoped that he was OK and nothing bad had come up. I checked my watch again; it was now 3:15 p.m. I decided to head out. I paid my tab and tipped the valet. Why the hell hadn't he contacted me?

I know what, I thought. I'll stop by his office. I drove to the building and parked. From the car, I called him again, on both his office line and his cell phone. No answer. Just before I could exit from my car, my phone rang.

"Hey, babe, it's me," Robert said. "Sorry. I got tied up and could not break away. I hope you have left."

Is he serious? I thought. Does he really think that I would continue to wait for him for almost two hours? "Yes, I left," I replied angrily. "What do you mean that you could not break away? Is this what we've come to, Robert? Lately, it just seems that things are going downhill in this marriage, and I don't like it!"

Robert interrupted. "Do you actually think that I'm doing this on *purpose*? I told you that I am *working*! And if you would just get something going for yourself, you would understand!"

I looked at the phone in disbelief. *He* had called *me* to invite me for lunch! "Are you crazy, Robert? You called me for lunch. Did you forget? You called me and asked if we could meet. You know what? I am ending this call before we say something we'll regret. Bottom line, Robert, you are in error for not being sensitive enough to call me rather than let me wait. That was wrong. So I will talk—"

"Look Mo-Monique, don't you hang up this phone. I am talking to you—"

I clicked the phone button to hang up. "Not anymore, Robert. Not anymore. You're not talking, and ain't nobody listening." Even as I hung up, I decided to wait to see if Robert was leaving the building or if I could see his truck in the area where he normally parked. My Robert was acting stranger than he had in years, and it was time that I paid some attention. I had always heard stories of how women had to spy on their significant others. This was something that I refused to do. But today, I felt in my heart that I needed to see if, indeed, something was going on. So I waited.

Just as I thought, he eventually walked out of the side door with a female I did not recognize. Of course, she could be a client. But since when did he personally walk a client to her car? He would make sure that security escorts the female clients— only if needed.

Robert exited his building with this tall, slender woman with ass for days hugged up. Laughing. What could be so damn funny? I thought. She rubbed his face, while stroking the beard I hated. Both of them, arms locked. Kissing. Gazing at each other.

I sat, watched, and waited. Hmm. A hug. Then he spotted me. I did try to duck. But why should I do that? I thought. For goodness sake, I was his wife; he was my husband. Unless things have changed, and I was the last person to know.

I sat and looked. My phone rang. "Why are you just sitting there?" Robert asked me. I politely hung up.

Days and then weeks went by with me waiting on dates and Robert eventually being a no-show. I refused to think anything of my husband other than that he was a hard worker and slightly insensitive. I kept telling myself to stay busy with school, to do projects in this big, lonely home. I could take a trip with a girlfriend, shop, do anything. I had the best, as Robert was a great provider, but I was lonely. Lonely as hell. I did not want to hang with girlfriends. I did not want to shop. I had a shoe closet and a closet for coats and purses; you name it, I had it. I wanted my man, but it seemed that my man no longer wanted me.

Winter had come, and soon, the holidays would be here. The last time the fireplace was lit was for the last romantic dinner he and I shared. I didn't light fires, no matter how cold it got outside.

We always decorated the house for the holidays. We would do this right before Thanksgiving. My family asked if we were doing anything that year. I said that we'd decided to travel and spend some quality time with each other in hopes of getting pregnant. This was a lie—the biggest one I'd ever told. But for the life of me, I couldn't allow my heart to grow cold—I loved Robert too much.

I had taken a leave of absence from the elementary school where I was a teacher. I could no longer put my heart and mind into teaching those beautiful kids—not when I was not enjoying life, not when I wanted a child of my own.

Robert never invited me to the apartment, although, he said that I could visit at any time. Isn't this a joint venture? I wondered. Robert said that when he was done with most of his cases, he would just crash there because he was so tired. He would often send me a text to wish me a good night and promise to stop by in the morning or afternoon to make sure that everything was OK at the house. I was lonely. Empty.

Before I headed over to the university one day, I drove by Robert's office. I had to see my husband, and this time, he was going to talk to me. I didn't care. I got out of my car to enter the building. The woman at the security desk looked at me and then looked down at the book she was reading. I got to his office. He was here. Finally, we saw each other. The same chick was there. She just gave me a faint smile and then put her head down and walked away.

"Come on in, sweetheart," Robert said. "How have you been? We are finally wrapping up this case just in time for Christmas. Are you hungry? Thirsty? Here, let me make you a cup of coffee. It's freezing out there. So what brings you by?"

I wanted to yell, scream, kick, and cry. I missed him. I loved him. But now, I hated him too. I hated who I was becoming: lonely and bitter. I was not sure about the bitter part, though. Was it because of another woman or the fact that Robert had left me but not officially?

"Robert, are we still married? I mean, you're the attorney. You have not been home…well, to the house…in almost two months now. If you no longer want to be with me, please say that."

Robert walked over and gave me the cup of coffee. "Here, drink. I made it just the way you like it. Now, no, we are not divorced or separated. I will be back home."

I took a sip of the coffee, and he was right: it was just the way I like it—black with sugar only. I peered over the cup. "Robert, I have been alone. You only text me to say good night. We are married. Don't you get that? And I've seen you several times with that woman. May I ask who she is?"

Robert sat next to me. "Babe, she's a client. Unfortunately, I am not at liberty to discuss anything more than that. I know that it does not look good. However, once this is over, you will see."

Robert stood and walked over to his office door, locking it. He unbuttoned his shirt and belt and walked back to me, "Now, you act like you miss me. Show me." Unbelievably, Robert took out his penis, expecting me to perform. But at that moment, I would have done anything to feel close to him. After all, a wife was supposed to please her husband, right? As I pulled him close to me, I looked up at him, and my eyes began to fill with tears.

Robert bent down and whispered, "It's going to be OK. Now, go on and show me just how much you miss me."

The ride home was different. Part of me felt happy because I'd seen my man. The other part felt like a fool.

I'd thought we were about to make love. Yes, in his office, but then I would stay, and we would go a few flights up to the apartment. It did not happen that way. Instead, once I was done with him, he zipped his pants up, kissed me on the cheek, and said he had to get back to work. He walked me to the elevator and told me to text him once I got home. As all of this played back in my mind, I began to cry. I was sobbing so loudly that at the traffic light, people in other cars were staring. I made it home and locked the doors. I went upstairs and showered.

The house was cold, but instead of heating the entire house, I lit the fireplace that was laid for a romantic evening. I put on cozy socks and snuggled up in front of it with a blanket and my tablet. I checked my email, reading and deleting them one by one. Then I noticed an e-mail from Professor Billingsley at Central University. I opened it, hoping that he was not about to pry, that he wasn't going to ask when I'd stop by or why I was avoiding any conversation with him.

But it was just a simple and sweet note. *Hey, how are you? Stay warm.*

Reading a note like that, I needed to stay warm. My heart was beginning to distance itself a little more each day from the man whom I'd thought would never hurt me.

I responded, *Hi, Professor. It is much too cold to request something impossible. I hope that you had a great semester and have a happy holiday. Monique*

I fell asleep in my chair. Every now and then, I awoke to find tears flowing down my cheeks. I prayed that these bad days and feelings would soon fade away.

I rose with the morning light, not realizing how long I'd slept. My tablet showed that I had five e-mails from the professor. Sleepy eyed but alert, I opened them one by one. Each one had a funny message to grab my attention. Instead of responding to his e-mails, I located the business card that he'd given me the first time we met. I decided to give him a morning call.

All professional, he answered, "Monroe Billingsley."

I decided to be a little playful. "Monroe," I said. "Monroe Billingsley, there are no classes today, for it is the weekend."

He paused for a moment. "Miss…I mean, *Mrs.* Sails? Is this you?"

I waited a moment before I responded. "Yes. How did you know?"

He cleared his throat. "I could never forget a voice as distinctive as yours."

Hmm, I thought. Robert had started complaining that my voice was whiny. "A distinctive voice?" I asked. "Are you saying that I am whiny?"

Laughter from the other end. "Why would you say that? No, I don't think so at all. You have a certain dialect with a Southern charm. But never whiny. How is it going? You must've fallen asleep."

I walked over to the window to peer into my driveway. "Yeah, I did. Yesterday was a rough day. Not such a good day. How have you been?"

"I've been well. I am looking forward to the break. Just for a while. What are your family's plans?"

I hesitated, rolling my eyes, before I answered. "Professor, I don't have any. This is the first time that I have no holiday plans. But I am willing to try something different this winter."

Hanging out with Monroe was beautiful. I was feeling like my old self but new. We shopped, hung out, and just had plain old fun. I had invested my past, present, and my future in Robert as my husband, and he had no plans to be with me. For whatever reason, he had a hard time being honest. He was somewhat controlling, which to me was not an issue, but dishonesty was a big issue. I was not rushing into something with Monroe. Our friendship was just that: a friendship. I had shared some things about Robert with Monroe but not all. One thing that I chose to do was not to be a victim. I should have seen through Robert and his foolish antics a long time ago. The house that Robert and I once shared was barely lived in. I spent most of my time at Monroe's. He was helping me to reinvent myself. But he assured me that taking steps toward a new relationship would be a process. My heart had grown calloused, and trust in others had gone out the door.

Months had gone by, and Robert had not called or had the decency to come back. To him, I was just a financial obligation. An employee but indirectly, I worked for him. Robert grew his practice, becoming one of the top firms in the city. In fact, he had become a "superlawyer" and one of the city's biggest advocates on social issues. That same woman—the one who hadn't dared to look at me—was with him. In the newspaper photos, there she would be, in the background. He was so controlling that she dared not stand by his side.

Me and my foolish heart. I'd wanted a baby with Robert so badly, but that dream had gone out the door as well. I could've filed for divorce on the grounds of abandonment, but I decided not to. I could bring him down for everything. But what would that prove? Absolutely nothing. At the end of the day, I would still be without him, feeling angry and hurt. Image had become everything to Robert and me. I'd lost myself in him years ago by building his dream and not seeking my own.

My lovemaking with Monroe meant more to him than it did to me. Because I was so calloused, sex was just a physical fulfillment rather than an emotional one. I couldn't let myself go. I refused to be played again. No way would I do that.

Monroe encouraged me to finish my classes and go back to teaching. He said that I should always follow my heart, and I was happiest when I was teaching the children. Monroe was in love with the idea of love and helping others to grow to their fullest potentials. I knew that I still had a soft spot for Robert. He was someone who, unfortunately, had become all about himself. But that did not stop me from loving him. Monroe would get so angry at times because he felt that I was a good person who was continuing to waste my heart on someone who was not worth it.

One day, Robert called and asked if we could meet. Lovingly, foolishly, I was excited to join him. We met at the

Intercontinental Hotel. This time, he beat me there and was waiting in the restaurant when I arrived. When I saw him, my heart immediately danced in sheer delight. Although I had broken away from him, I still arrived looking as beautiful as I could. Every strand of hair was in place. I wore my best fragrance. Was this to get back at him and bait him by implying, "Aha, look what you're missing"? Certainly not. I was not petty. He was still my husband. Although I'd sort of moved on, my ears and heart were itching to hear what he would say. Robert stood up as I walked into the restaurant.

"Hi, Monique," he said. "Please sit down. You're looking nice today. I know that this conversation is long overdue."

I was lost and without any words. He motioned for the waiter to come over and pour some champagne. I couldn't help but ask, "What are we celebrating?"

I continued to look at him and allowed him to do the talking. "I know that a year ago, I did not handle things very nicely while I was trying to get myself set up. The apartment, being MIA, all of that. I am here to say that I am sorry. I am sorry, Monique. I apologize for hurting you and causing you grief. It will never happen again. I have been so selfish. Very selfish. Tonight, if I could just enjoy the comfort of an old friend-lover, wife. Please, can we just enjoy the evening? Can you please forgive me?"

He held up his glass and motioned for me to do the same. "Today, we celebrate fresh, new beginnings," he said. "The cold, cold season is almost behind us. Let's forgive each other and move forward. Can we, Monique? Move forward? Cheers."

"Cheers," I said, nodding. We clicked our flutes together.

We drank and ate so much. It was indeed a memorable night. Somehow, I ended up in room 1215 with this man. I had no intention of allowing myself to be physical with him again. But this was unexpected. The way Robert touched me was just like old times. My phone beeped and buzzed. Monroe's number popped up on the hour. Eventually, I shut the dang thing off.

I did not care. Again, I was in my husband's presence, and he wanted a fresh start. In the morning, we got up and put our robes on. He ordered room service. We made love again and again. He had three dozen roses brought in. I wasn't sure of the significance of the number of stems, but I did not care. He was being thoughtful. My heart was beginning to warm again.

There was a knock on the door when Robert was in the shower. He yelled, "Monique, can you get that?"

I fastened my robe. "Sure, got it." Now, who could this be?

I opened the door to a gentleman, nicely dressed. "Monique Sails?" he asked.

I pushed my hair behind my ears. "Yes, I'm Monique Sails."

The man handed me a gold envelope. "You just got served. Thank you and good day."

I quickly opened the envelope. Served? By whom? The envelope contained divorce papers. That tricky son of a b**ch!

Someone was at the door again. I opened the door forcefully. This time, it was a police officer and hotel security. Did he actually think that I would cause a scene?

"Robert, you went through a lot just to tell me good-bye."

The police officer entered the room. "Ma'am, please get dressed and grab your things so that you can leave peacefully."

For some reason, the tears would not stream. I could not cry. "OK," I said. "Let me put on my clothes. I will leave. Robert, why the three dozen roses? What did that mean?"

He walked toward me. "The three times that I allowed myself to be touched by you: the night we planned to go out, the day you came by my office, and this, this good-bye. Here's three hundred thousand to pay you off so that you never contact me again. I am moving on, and I am expecting to have a son and a new wife. It's over, Monique. I don't know why I held on this long. I thought that maybe you would have had sense enough to move on, but you didn't. I fell out of love with you years ago. You had no more get-up-and-go. You were just too involved, Monique. Too smart for your own good, but you continued to settle. It's over. The house is up for sale too. I know that you haven't been there lately. I hear that you have your little professor to keep you warm. I hope that he has enough room. But if he doesn't, you have some monies to jump-start a new life. So good-bye, Monique."

The officer and security guard looked at him and then, sadly, at me. I was numb. I felt useless. Empty. Cold and void.

I had the valet bring my car around. All I could do was sit for a moment. Monroe had left a ton of messages. I listened to each one of them. They went from "Where are you?" to "I hope you're OK" to "This is stupid." He was all over the place too. I decided to dial him, but when he said hello, I could barely speak.

"Monroe," I whispered.

We both held our phones in silence.

He decided to speak up. "Listen, Monique, if you've been with Robert, don't come this way. I mean, I've been here for you. I've compromised with you when I know that you didn't deserve it. I've been more than patient with you. So please, don't say another word if this has something to do with your husband."

Desperately grasping for words, I stammered, "No, he's my ex—I mean—he just—please, Monroe, listen to what I have to say. Please."

Monroe hung up, and I never saw or talked to him again either.

Two years went by. For years, I wanted love, but I did not love myself. Turns out that Robert did remarry, two more times, and fathered four girls. I finally gave birth to a son. I named him Pharus, which is short for Pharaoh. I named him Pharus in hopes that his life would be the opposite of that of a king with a hardened heart.

These days, I could only do the best that I knew how. I loved my son, but I didn't know whom I was looking at because I didn't know who his father was.

Knocks on the door and unexpected mail deliveries leave me shaken. A year ago, I received a letter from the Centers for Disease Control and Prevention telling me to be tested

frequently for HIV and hepatitis. Rumor had it that the professor preyed on students at Central, both females and males.
Lately, he was nowhere to be found. As for me, as many times
as the season changed, I owed it to myself to hold on to what I
knew—to never trust or forgive. Mistakes of loving others like
Robert and trusting Monroe more than loving myself was a
huge mistake. I now held on this for me and my son. I no longer
wrote in a journal. Journals were only for those who needed
to reflect. Someday, my bitterness will be released, but until
then, the old Monique is dead and silent.

Matters of a Man's Heart

On the way home from church, Jaiden and I had the worst fight. I never thought that as a man of the cloth, I would have the worst marriage ever.

When I met Jaiden, she was closed off from the world. Quiet. Meek. Never wanting things that others had and a woman after my heart. Then she became the First Lady, and I was pretty sure she was not ready for this role. Instead, she became a monster, and we fought and fought.

It was snowing that night, and I was tired because we had been at church and around members the entire day. Jaiden wanted some sort of extra recognition and wanted to be the center of attention, as always. This time, she went too far. As I was driving, the heifer put her hands on me. She yelled and stamped her feet. Then she flicked her finger on the side of my face, and from anger, I must have blacked out.

The next day, I woke up bandaged, one leg in a sling, and a morphine pump hooked up to my arm. I could vaguely hear the slow beeps of the heart monitor. As I tried to adjust, a nurse scribbled info on the whiteboard. I tried to get her attention, wondering what had happened and where Jaiden was. The nurse came over and asked if I wanted to sit up; she said to do it slowly. As she gave me a sip of water, I glanced at her name badge: "Bailey." I grabbed her arm, clearing my throat. "Ex-excuse me, Ms. Bail-leah."

She quickly corrected me. "It's Bay-lee. You've been out for a while. How are you feeling?"

How I was feeling? I thought. I began to ask her how I got there and where my wife was. Bailey stated that I was at County General Hospital, and I had been transported there via ambulance. I rubbed my forehead. I sort of remembered what was happening right before I blacked out: I was in the car, arguing with Jaiden, and then mysteriously, I ended up here, alone.

Bailey said she would get the doctor so that a family member could come to speak to me.

I thought, What does she mean, a family member? Where is my dang wife? Why isn't she here already? Maybe she's here, and we got separated or…Lord, something tragic happened. I really began to fear the worst. I braced myself and began to pray. I prayed that she was here and was not injured, or worse, *dead*. I hoped that she was downstairs in the cafeteria or lobby. Lord, please let her not have suffered any harm.

Tears began to stream down my face because fear quickly overtook me. The nurse entered the room with a physician. In slow motion, I waited to hear, Sorry, Jaiden didn't make it. Was I crazy? Did I want this for her? Did this fear wash over me due to the anger that took place in the car? Had I wanted her to die? Oh Lord, please forgive me for my thoughts.

The physician approached me. "Mr. Mitchell, how are you feeling today, sir? I am sure you have some questions concerning your stay, and I am sure, too, that you see that you took a pretty good injury. Your left leg is broken, and you have a contusion on the knee. The soreness you feel is what we call soft-tissue injury. This resulted when the car flipped, according to the police and medics who brought you here."

I hit the pump so that more medicine would hit my aching body and started to speak with the physician. "Thank you, Doctor, for this information. I am most interested in knowing where my wife is. Is she next door or in another unit?"

The physician looked at the medical chart and notes. "Mr. Mitchell, we don't show...Or at least, there is no report included on the chart that your wife or any passengers were in the accident with you. I mean—"

I interrupted him. "I'm sorry. This is impossible. I mean, I was in the car with my wife, and we argued. We screamed. This is impossible!"

The nurse came over to me and nodded to the physician. "Mr. Mitchell, we want to give you a sedative so that we can keep you calm. Your blood pressure is elevated, and we would like to keep it down. Do you have any more questions, Mr. Mitchell?"

I could feel the medicine enter my veins from the IV, and slowly, calmly, I drifted off to sleep.

My brother and his wife periodically checked on me and brought me home from the hospital a week after the accident. I missed our home, and it was still a mystery as to what happened that almost-fateful night. I eventually learned how to walk with crutches. The doctor stated that it would be a while before the cast could be removed. I learned that while I was in the hospital, I'd announced that I was about to take a sabbatical from the ministry and had expressed thoughts of leaving as a pastor altogether. Was this the reason for that argument in the car?

No one could explain the disappearance of Jaiden. It was almost as if she had evaporated, or maybe I was so angry with her that I made it up in my head that she was there. There was no proof that we were together that night. It was true that I was driving home from church, and it was indeed a snowy night. But she was my wife. Why hadn't she come to see about me? During my stay at the hospital, my heart began to harden. As a wife, why wasn't she there? Furthermore, where the hell was she now? I thanked my brother and sister-in-law for their acts of kindness and told them that I really wanted to be alone.

I walked to our bedroom to get some rest. Now in my cold home, alone, I had to gather the pieces of a puzzle that I no longer could grasp. I could not jog any memory of what happened. Our his-and-her closet was half empty—or, as Jaiden would consider it, half full. We would argue about that too. Which way was the correct way of viewing things in the world, half empty or half full? I sat down on the bed and grabbed my pain meds. Everything in my body seemed to ache. I walked to the bathroom, got a glass of water, and noticed that it seemed that Jaiden had packed her things quickly. I flipped two pills into my mouth and gulped some water. As I swallowed, I noticed a book, a journal, on the floor. When I picked it up, a picture fell out. It was an ultrasound picture of a baby.

My heart began to race. We argued and argued because I really wanted a baby, and she always firmly stated that she was not ready. The picture, folded in half, was marked Jaiden Brooks, which was her maiden name. As I flipped through the pages in the journal, I saw that the last entry was dated a week before our accident. I was exhausted, but after seeing this picture, I struggled to stay awake. I tried to sit up in bed, but my eyes were too heavy. The painkillers were beginning to take effect. I lay on the pillow, trying to focus and recall that week, particularly the last day I thought we had been together. A business card was stuck between the pages. "Family Care Services," I whispered. "So, she was going to abort the baby..." I flipped through a few more pages and found a place where she had written that things were too difficult without knowing who the father is. Why did I fear this? Why did I suddenly feel distrust? I felt vulnerable.

"What in the heck does she mean 'who the father is'? This can't be...Naw. Naw, man..." My heart ached. I kept reading, and each page was crazier than the last. However, I could no longer resist the euphoria of the pain pills and the comfort of my own bed. I pulled the covers up, and slowly I felt myself drift off to sleep. A sound, peaceful sleep, so sleepy...finally. But as I drifted off...no Jaiden...now this journal...a baby... mine. These thoughts entered my dreams. As I felt myself drift further, I felt as if someone were watching me...

A year and six months passed, and still there was no sign of Jaiden. As for me, I had to move on. It was obvious that she'd packed her things and left not a single piece of clothing, just the journal. I reported her missing; the detectives felt there was no sign of foul play. Based on what the police stated, there were no indications that she had been there at the scene of the accident. It hurt badly that she would just take off like that. I struggled in my prayers to God. What did I do that was so horrendous that she would leave without a trace? Then there was the picture of a baby and the clinic's card. None of this made any sense. I guess it was all timing. In one of nightstand drawers, I came across a picture of Jaiden, young and full of God's promises. She was so beautiful, but things changed when I decided to step down, and we argued about starting a family. Jaiden felt that having a baby soon—only two years after we married—would ruin things between us. And my leaving the church was another fretful thing. She became worried about our finances. I felt as though the church itself was no longer focused on God's plans. The board had a different vision of the direction in which the church should go, so I felt that it was best that I resign. As I studied the photograph, at times I still had the eerie feeling of being watched. At times, I thought maybe I was going crazy.

I glanced in the mirror. "Hey, you! What are you doing? Are you hungry?" I said, quickly putting the photo of Jaiden in another drawer. "Sweetheart, how many times have I asked you to stop sneaking up on me, huh? And don't give me the puppy-dog look. I love you, you know that? I love you so very much, and nothing or no one can take you away from me. You were here, Monica, when no one else seemed to care. I know things moved fast for us. However, love has no timing. Do you agree, no timing?" I wiped the tears from my new wife's face.

Monica was there for me. In the weeks that I struggled to care for myself, she was one of the church members who came over and took care of me with no motive but love itself. Monica understood the loss that I felt and was still experiencing. Jaiden broke my heart and left me. She left me with nothing, no words, no good-bye. She was just gone. Or maybe I had not accepted that she was dead. But things happened for a reason. I had a new woman in my life, and Monica loved me unconditionally.

I rubbed her belly and rocked her from behind, looking at us in the mirror. "I can't wait for our baby to get here. He's going to be nice and strong."

Monica laughed. "It could be a girl, and you continue to believe it's a—"

I turned Monica to face me. "God showed me that it"—I pointed to her belly—"is a boy."

"Yeah, OK. God could tell me the same, don't you think? And don't start that man stuff either. Now come on and eat."

Yes, I moved on, and obviously, so did Jaiden.

Restoration is something that mortal man can't ever do alone without the help of God. When you are empowered by those in your congregation or your town, power can sometimes be abused. For the last year, I've lived with questions and doubt and wanting revenge. That frightful ride that Daniel and I shared turned my life upside down. As the car flipped down the snowy embankment, I knew that our lives were over. I prayed and prayed that someone would see us and rescue us before the snowstorm moved in. When the car stopped, I could unstrap the seat belt from myself.

We had landed on the roof of the glorified and praised car that the members thought was a blessing. One part of me was happy to see the car destroyed. That would be one less association with the church. I walked over to the driver's side, but I could not open the door. I felt blood running down my cold cheeks. Apparently, I cut my head. I went back to my side of the car to contact 911 through OnStar, but there was no service because we had flipped so far down the hill. I scrambled for my phone, and I tried again to contact 911. Still no service. Finally, the blue and red lights of the police appeared at the top of the hill. I felt cold and warm at the same time. A shadow stood over me, and I fainted.

I remember waking up in Creekside Manor as a Jane Doe. Over the months, I moved to a rehab center for special care of my right leg and back. There was a gentleman at my side every day. His name was Messiah. Messiah brought flowers and took care of me alongside the care team and specialists. The doctors in the hospital stated that I suffered from post-traumatic stress disorder, and they made notes based on only what I could share with them. I was admitted with no identification, no family, and no cell phone even though I knew I'd used one to call 911 during the accident. Many things did not add up, and that frustrated me. As the days progressed, so did my memory. Each day, I would get up and perform physical therapy to strengthen my leg and align my back. Messiah would be there to assist me, along with the therapist.

"Messiah, you have been a great person throughout my ordeal. Would you happen to know anything? I mean, anything about me?"

He walked me out to the courtyard, and thankfully, it was a beautiful day.

How did I get here? Oh yes, love. Love for a man who belonged to me and not to her. I would do anything in the world for Daniel. For years, I watched Jaiden walk proudly into church each Sunday and for Bible study with Daniel. I felt so bad for him…getting up before the congregation and soliciting prayers for his wife to conceive a child. All the ladies and I knew that she wasn't ready. It was a wasted prayer. I believed that ladies should always give a man what he wanted to keep him, and guess what? I was the winner, and she was the loser.

I made my way in and did so quickly. I helped him to correct all his wrongs of the church first, so that I became the First Lady. And to add a blessing to the congregation, I conceived a baby. Once I was done having the first baby, I would bless him with another and another. Daniel's problem with the board stemmed from the fact that he was too "caught up" in loving the wrong woman. Jaiden, perfect Jaiden. She didn't fit, nor did she belong. I watched Daniel and perfect Jaiden Mitchell for years.

The news traveled fast the night of the accident. I had followed them out of curiosity about what our tithes and offerings were paying for. I never expected the car to flip over. I gasped when I saw it. I stayed to the side and dialed 911. I could not bear it if anything happened to Daniel. The emergency team brought Daniel up on the stretcher with an oxygen mask over his face. I exhaled because this indicated that he was still alive. He kept mumbling, "My wife…Jaiden."

I wanted to run over there and stop him from talking. I looked back down the hill, and I could see the light of a phone, which told me that Jaiden was somewhere in the vicinity. Luckily for me, my brother Al showed up at the scene and directed the search party. Al asked what I saw. I told him that the car kept swerving and then it flipped, just like that, and went down the embankment. I saw Jaiden's phone and her things, and I wanted so desperately to go then. If I could dash down the hill and grab some of her loosed items that I assumed fell out of the car and hide them in my purse. The snow started to come down harder. If only I could persuade my brother and the others that we needed to leave before the storm got dangerous so that I could grab what I could. I did not want anyone to find Jaiden. I explained to my brother that it appeared that Pastor Mitchell was traveling alone. Besides, no one at church was sure of how they'd traveled that night. Jaiden did her own thing, at times riding solo or leaving before service was over.

If I could get past this night, I thought, it would look as if she just went off on one of her rants, as she'd done before, and left.

The rescue team headed back up the hill, and everyone took off. I stood there, looking around. Where could she be hiding?

When the paramedics and police departed, I figured that this would be a great time to head toward the house. I rummaged through her purse and located her license. I typed the address into my phone and proceeded to move forward. The Mitchell home was everything that I imagined it would be—decorated in warm colors, clean, and welcoming. There were a few things that I would change. "I will. I will change that later," I said to myself. I moved to the bedroom and went to her closet. "Man, this woman has everything." I went over to her nightstand and voilà! A journal. Jaiden did not write much in it. However, I did notice a sonogram of a baby. "She's pregnant? Ugh, not for long."

I located a pen, and I began to write some nonsense in the journal. He won't know the difference. I did this purposely so Mitchell or someone would see this once Mitchell returns home from the hospital. I wrote about not wanting to be pregnant and, as a side note, scribbled the name of a clinic in town that was known for performing abortions. I placed the picture right on the page with the address. I moved the journal to a more suspicious place; in her closet on the floor. "Well," I said aloud, "it's got to look like she came back and moved her things." I began to pull down some of her clothes. I could not remove everything. I just grabbed a few things out of each section of the closet—pants, shoes, you name it. I left the house nicely secured and thought about my plans.

After Messiah told me everything He knew, my heart broke. Daniel never came back to look for me. He should have known that things were moving much too fast between that Monica and him. I hoped he got what he deserved. Messiah said that He could not prove it, but He felt that Monica was the source of all the chaos from the accident. How did He end up there at the scene? Messiah told me that He had always prayed for the pastor and his family—me. It wasn't any of His business, but He sensed that there would always be something wrong. The news had traveled fast that night, so Messiah came up the back roads on the other side of the embankment, and He found me. He took me to Creekside Manor, which was a small hospital, and there, He and others took care of me. It was at Creekside Manor that I really learned the true meaning of forgiveness. I forgave, and I moved forward. This would be a process. I knew that at times things would present themselves to me, and those emotions would resonate all over again. I lost our baby. I had an ultrasound done in my maiden name due to privacy concerns. I wanted to tell him so badly, but he was too concerned about the church and what he looked like in front of others rather than about his relationship with God. All that I had left was my new friend.

Messiah reminded me that it was our responsibility and special right, that God our Father had granted to us to forgive and move from our past. I thought of Ephesians 4:22–24: "You were taught, regarding your former way of life, to put off your old self, which is being corrupted by its deceitful desires; to be made new in the attitude of your minds; and to put on the new self, created to be like God in true righteousness and holiness." I continued to heal as the newly created Jaiden and loved myself more. As for Messiah and me, we became the closest of friends. I prayed for Daniel and Monica, and I only wished them the best.

I was excited that Monica was about to deliver our son. I called all the elders and told them that we were about to welcome my first son into the world. Monica had called a few of the sisters from the church and, of course, the intercessory team. Her mom and family stayed in the waiting room as the intercessory team prayed my son through his new journey. Baby Jordan was born within a few hours. He weighed a whopping nine pounds. We watched the nurse take blood from Jordan for lab tests. We kissed him all over his little hands and feet.

The doctor had requested blood samples from us to determine which of Jordan's parents had the gene for sickle cell or the disease itself. Jordan's lab results came in, and he required mild treatment. I would do anything for my son, so we both got our arms ready to have blood drawn to help our son. They brought Jordan back into the room, and we were filled with joy. We passed him around, and church members took pictures and uploaded them on social media.

Then the doctor came in and asked that everyone step out of the room. "Mr. and Mrs. Mitchell, we ran the test several times to determine who carries the gene for sickle cell anemia. It is very important that we test both parents and educate you both early. However, we did not find the gene in either of you. If the child has sickle cell, at least one parent, if not both, would have the gene or the trait. So we also ran another test just to rule out any additional variables. We know, Mrs. Mitchell, that you are the mother; you gave birth. But Mr. Mitchell, the lab does not show that you are a donor match or that any of your DNA matches Jordan's."

My heart dropped. This was too much, after the events of the last year or so. What had I done to be forsaken? First, my wife leaves me—or she's dead—and now my new son—no, my *wife's* son…

Monica began to weep when I asked her to explain. She just could not. There was a tap on the door, and I snatched open the door and shouted, "Not right—"

There, on the other side of the door, was Messiah and the most beautiful woman in the world, holding a bouquet of flowers, Jaiden Mitchell.

The Inheritance

While at the attorney's office, signing papers related to my deceased great-grandmother's estate, my emotions were bittersweet. Although I had never met Fannie Lou French, I had heard or read many wonderful things about her. Fannie was a slave and endured many hardships. The stories were frightful; some were unbelievable. During the latter years of her life, Fannie managed to inherit more than ten acres of land, which included a lake stocked with fish, a lake house with four bedrooms, and stables. Rumor had it that there had been several owners of the property, and these people had mysteriously vanished. Once the people vanished, rumors began that there were papers tucked inside a vault and that the last owner—Mr. Jude Willoughby—had willed the estate to Fannie.

I benefited because most of my family members' whereabouts were unknown or they were deceased. However, one of my great-aunts was gracious enough to locate me and tell me about the signing and the inheritance.

As I signed each page, I lovingly looked at my husband, Charles. Charles was a fair—skinned man, tall with gray curly hair. He was a few years older than me, and I loved Charles to the moon and back. We'd never had much, but this would surely jump-start our lives, provide a new beginning. I noticed how the attorneys were looking at me. One had a wary look, and the other, an expression of pity. I glanced back at them with a faint, uncertain smile—maybe this was not a good idea. But why would it not be? It was a *great* thing to inherit the land, a home with a lake. I dismissed those thoughts and continued to flip through the pages.

"There, Mrs. Vincent. This is the last document, and the property is yours."

My heart pounded, each beat bouncing off the walls and bookshelves. The keys were reluctantly passed to me, and I could faintly hear or read the attorney's mind. *Don't go to that property.*

I snatched the keys, thanked them, and walked as fast as I could to the car. The attorneys came out on the porch and watched us go up the driveway. Looking back, I had the most eerie feeling. It was as if they knew something about my past or maybe my future.

It was moving day, and our move was easy, considering that most of the rooms in the home were already furnished. Charles wasn't a fan of the decor; however, for me, it was perfect. As we finished putting our clothes away, we found a box. "Hmm, someone did not remove all the personal belongings from this closet." I decided to look in the box and blew off some of the dust.

At the bottom of the box, under old papers, was a journal with a locket. I shuffled through some of the pages and then moved to the papers. There were pictures of a woman who appeared to be my great-great-grandmother. Fannie was a woman of beauty. She had the appearance of a Native American mixed with African American: long, black hair, with very prominent cheekbones. The pictures were dated from the early 1800s to the present, 2017. How could that be? I continued to go through the pictures, and I discovered marriage certificates bearing Fannie's name along with those of various husbands. The last certificate showed Jude Willoughby as a husband—a skinny white man with blue eyes and dark curly hair.

I ran downstairs, where I found Charles with my aunt Viola and her stepdaughter Cameron. "Oh, I didn't realize…Aunt Viola, I didn't know you were coming. You did not have to drive that distance. You should have at least called."

Charles began to speak. "Honey, I called your aunt to keep you company while I worked on some of the things on the property. I hope—"

Aunt Viola grabbed my hands. "Sweetheart, I am sorry I did not speak to you personally. The blame for this is mine. I had asked Charles to keep it a surprise that I was coming to visit. You remember your cousin Cameron?"

I hesitated before I responded. I could not understand for the life of me why Aunt Viola continued to parade this girl around as if she were her own. Aunt Viola and her ex had divorced more than five years ago, and Cameron was trouble.

She had caused my aunt Viola to make many trips to the hospital stemming from high blood pressure and even a heart attack.

"Yes, I remember Cameron."

Cameron rubbed her hands on her jeans, extending herself to hug me. "It is good to see you again, Shannon. I hope that we can become closer during our stay here."

Stay? I thought. Wow, no one bothered to include me in this charade. "Ah, Charles, may I see you in the kitchen?"

Charles began to rub my shoulders as he reminded me not to become upset over their visit. "Remember what the doctor said, sweetie. Try not to get upset over frivolous stuff. Look, they're family. We need them here. There's a lot of property to cover, and I would like for us to get settled in so that we can enjoy the lake. OK? Agree?"

Charles was right. I needed to maintain control and stop sweating the small stuff. However, a courtesy call would have been appreciated. I returned to the living room, not realizing that I still had the pictures in my back pocket.

Aunt Viola looked at me. "Shannon, what's that in your pocket?"

I turned around acting as if she didn't realize the pictures my pocket. "Oh, I found some pictures of Fannie in a box upstairs in the closet."

Aunt Viola started to walk toward me, reaching for the pictures. "Let me see, Shannon, what you're talking about." She took the pictures and fumbled through some of them. Then she placed them all in her purse. In confusion, I looked at her to understand why she put them into her purse rather than handing them back to me. For a few seconds, our eyes would not leave each other's. I did not know what else to do so I decided to head upstairs and noticed that the box was gone!

I started to fill up with anxiety because I knew that I had left the box there. I went through my purse, grabbed my pills, took a drink of water, and lay down. Maybe, just maybe, my mind was beginning to play a trick on me. First the sudden visit. Then the pictures and the disappearance of the box. Was someone trying to keep something from me? The attorneys... wow. If you could have seen the look of fear in their eyes. It was as if they were secretly pleading with me not to come to this place.

Suddenly, I heard people talking. I sat up in bed and leaned toward the vents to listen. The voices seemed to come from somewhere in the house. I thought I heard a man whispering and a woman in some hot rage. I got up and ran down the steps. I saw Aunt Viola in the kitchen. "Is everything OK, baby?" she asked. "I thought that maybe you were upstairs taking a nap."

I found myself having difficulty responding to Aunt Viola. I felt uneasy about her visit so soon after I received this property. Did she come to get a piece of the pie and do something underhanded? No, no. She was my mother's sister, for heaven's sake. Either I was overwhelmed, or my Xanax had taken effect. "Do you know where Charles is? I thought that I heard a man's voice and..."

Cameron entered the room. "Hey, cousin," she said, hugging me. "How was your nap?"

I looked at Cameron fearfully while backing away from her. "I did not take a nap. Where have you been? Are you sleeping with my husband? You, you—"

Aunt Viola jumped to her feet. "Chile, what has gotten into you? Why would you say such a thing to Cameron? Charles is not here."

I stormed out the door. The Jeep was gone. I went back into the house, ran past Aunt Viola and Cameron, and locked myself in my room. My heart started to race. I then dashed for the closet to look for the box again, and there it was. I began pulling my clothes and shoes from the closet. Surely, someone was watching me. Was there someone else in my home?

I pulled my phone out of my purse. "Shoot! No signal." This was not good. I changed into my sneakers to go for a walk. Perhaps that would clear my head. I made sure that I was quiet as I carried the box out of the back door. The lake looked so peaceful. I sat on the bench and started going through the box again. "Someone was committing fraud against Fannie," I said to myself. One document was an appraisal of the home and land that totaled $1.5 million. "One million dollars," I whispered. There it was: Willoughby's signature and next to it, what appeared to be the signature of Fannie Lou Willoughby.

"What in heavens?" I opened the journal. My Fannie described how she was beaten almost daily. She wrote about the many babies she lost due to the hardship of working on this land and the overseer's mistreatment. "Hmm, this property was a plantation and—"

"Shannon, what are you doing?"

The voice came from behind me. I scrambled to put the documents back into the box.

"What is that, sweetheart?" Charles asked.

I was hesitant to answer. "It's nothing. Where did you go?"

Charles walked toward me, and I stepped back. "What's wrong?" he asked. "You seem jumpy. Did you rest?"

"Actually, I did not. I began to hear strange voices and moaning from the vent in the master. I panicked, ran downstairs, and there was Cameron. And I—I accused her of sleeping with you." I felt ashamed and embarrassed.

Charles did not say anything. He put his arms around me, and we headed back toward the house. Unfortunately, Aunt Viola and Cameron were out on the front porch, pretending to be concerned.

Cameron began to speak. "Shan——"

I put my hand up and shook my head, not now. I did not want to hear anything she had to say.

Charles, kind and loving husband that he was, started a bubble bath for me. The water was perfect. I got in to soak. As I leaned back against the cold porcelain, the lights went out. I stood and wrapped a towel around myself, preparing to yell to Charles to check the fuse box. As I got out of the tub, I could sense movement or someone's presence from the closet. I ran quickly to see if I could catch a glimpse of the individual who was trying to scare me. Nothing. And then the lights came back on.

That was it for me. I put on some clean clothes and ran downstairs. "Charles, I am leaving. Once you and the rest of the clowns in this house decide to stop playing games and trying to scare me, let me know." I grabbed my keys, darted to the car, and drove off.

At midnight, Cameron left the house, and she was gone for hours. She knew it was time for Charles and her to make a move to get rid of Aunt Viola. Cameron went to Viola's room to give her something to drink laced with sleeping pills. A little while later, Cameron knocked on her door. "Aunt Viola, you are OK in there?"

No answer.

"Aunt Viola," Cameron gasped. "Charles! Charles!" Charles ran up the stairs. "Aunt Vi-Viola, she's not breathing. There's blood."

"Where is your phone, Cameron? We need to call 911. Someone has come in and done this to her, if it wasn't you. It certainly wasn't me."

"Where is my phone? Ooh, just please, breathe. No service. Charles, I can't get any service! Try your phone!"

"If you can't get any service, then neither can I," Charles responded angrily. "What happened? You were only supposed to give her sleeping pills, not make her bleed."

Cameron started to pace. "I didn't do this. I came down the hall, and there she was. In a p-pud-puddle of b-blood... Lying there! What are we going to do?"

Charles hugged Cameron tightly, fearing that someone else was in the house. "I betcha it's that crazy Shannon. She pretended to leave and learned some other way to enter the house. She was at the lake for a long time. I stood in the woods and watched her."

Cameron dried her face. "But why would she kill her aunt?"

A large crash sounded downstairs. Charles grabbed his gun.

"Who's there?" he yelled. "I have a loaded gun, and I am not afraid to use it. Stay back, Cameron."

Charles searched the house to learn that a tree had fallen through the kitchen window. He ran back up the stairs. "Cameron, phew, that was close. It was a tree. Cameron. Cameron? Where did she go?"

Charles saw a shadow dart across the room. Three shots rang out. POW, POW, POW. Then a thump as something hit the floor. Charles scrambled over and flipped the body with his foot. "Oh no! It's Cameron! No, baby. Wake up. You can't die on me!"

Charles listened for a heartbeat. It was there, but it was faint. He headed to the bathroom to wash his hands. While washing his bloodstained hands, he looked into the mirror. Then he turned to the vanity closet for a towel, and when he turned back, someone was standing behind him. He turned around, yelling in doomed horror. Suddenly, Charles disappeared.

I miss Charles, and I should not have left, I thought as I drove. If I had known better, I would have stayed to get answers. In my heart of hearts, Cameron could not be trusted. My aunt Viola endured so much with Cameron and her family. I am going back home to make up with Charles.

I parked my car and walked toward the house. Everything looked so peaceful and quiet. "Hello! Good morning!" I called. "Where is everybody?"

I noticed a trail of blood on the wall and stairs. I ran into the kitchen and grabbed a knife before climbing the stairs. "Hello, Aunt Vi…Oh no, who did this?" I looked over and saw Cameron and her long hair covered in a puddle of blood. She appeared to have been shot. Did Cameron and Charles have a fight? He was the only one with a gun.

"Argh! Stop shaking. Where is my phone?" I walked around until I got reception. Finally! "Yes, 911? Please send the police to 760 Shady Grove Lane. Someone has been shot and/or killed. Hurry!"

I walked down the hall looking for Charles. "Charles, where are you? Honey, we can talk if you did this. Come out. The police are on their way."

Someone appeared behind me. "It's good that they're on the way, Shannon."

I spun around and pointed the knife at the stranger. "Who are you? What do you want?"

The bony, scraggly man started laughing. "You thought you were going to sashay your high tail in here just like that and take what belongs to my family? Your great-great grandmother was a weirdo, and so was everyone after that. Cameron, she was for hire until that bomb of a husband of yours shot her.

They've been fooling around forever. The plan was to prove that you are crazy and have you committed. However, nope, nope. Your aunt had to get her nose in everything and meddle. I'll be damned if we pass all this land over to someone like you."

I kept the knife pointed at the stranger. Then I began to recognize his face from the pictures in the box. "Hey, you're Willoughby's grandson, Dan Willoughby! Why are you here? And where is my husband?"

Willoughby darted toward me. "Now you want to call that loose cannon your husband? Look, Shannon, we can make this easy. All you have to do is—"

The police burst into the house. "Ma'am, put down the knife. Put. Down. The. Knife. Or we will shoot."

Shannon dropped the knife.

"Officer," Dan said, "I heard there was some sort of disturbance here on my property, and I guess that these people were partying or something. Basically, they're trespassing. I found her, and she has a knife. Plus, two people are dead."

The officers turn toward me.

"Officers, this is my house," I said. "I just inherited it a week ago. My husband, Charles, and I moved in, and my aunt..." I began to weep.

"Ma'am, please give us your full name. Where is your husband now?"

I knelt on the floor. "My name is Shannon Vincent. And I don't know. I don't know where he is. I came back home. We had a big fi—"

Dan stepped in front of me. "Told you, Officers. There was some sort of commotion going on. No husband. No proof. She probably killed him too."

The officers began to handcuff me. "Shannon Vincent, you are under arrest. You have the right to remain silent…"

I began to fight. "No, no. You have this all wrong. Please don't do this."

The officers led me to the police car and drove me to the jail to be booked.

Dan Willoughby called in a crew to see if Charles could be located and to clean the house. He had the crew clean every crevice of the property as it searched. Dan had known all along that he would get the property that once belonged to his family. But the box that Shannon had found in the closet contained evidence that would prove he was a fraud. It would be hard for Shannon to prove her innocence now, with no family to help her and no alibi. Dan went back to the master bedroom to look for the box.

"Shoot," he said. "It's gone. Now, where is it?" He searched and searched for the box. Dan had no idea that this charade would turn out like this. He'd tussled with Aunt Violet the fretful evening before with no intention of hurting her. He'd just wanted to scare her away. Now, he felt a sudden chill as he remembered the stories that his grandfather told. He said that old lady Fannie had vowed that her spirit would never go away, that this was her father's land, and we'd stolen it from him.

Dan also recalled rumors that people who fished on the other side of the lake would see Fannie walking through the garden and stables. That kind of stuff only becomes true if you believe in it, he told himself. The thing that I believe to be the truth is that this property is mine, and it belonged to my ancestors—not to Fannie's and not to Shannon or anyone else.

Dan went into the bathroom to wash his face with cold water. He noticed that the power kept tripping the fuse. "Need to get an electrician here tomorrow," he said to himself. Dan stood up from the sink and reached for a towel. He let out a loud scream when the body of Charles Vincent fell out of the closet.

No one knew why Dan Willoughby died. Some say that he died of a heart attack. When the cleaning crew found him, his eyes were white and his face looked as if he'd seen a ghost. They also found the box with his fingers clasped around the handle. Somehow, Shannon was set free from jail. Some say she was extremely lucky. Shannon felt as though she'd been visited by an angel. The detectives reviewed the papers that were in the box and deemed that Dan Willoughby and Cameron had defrauded Shannon and her family. Shannon put the property up for sale and collected more than two million dollars. In honor of Shannon's family, the property was named Fannie's Bed and Breakfast. Visitors often traveled to Oxford, Georgia, for the thrill of hearing the tales of the great Fannie Lou French. Many visitors were obsessed with the bathroom and the vanity closet, which was now boarded up. But you could only see what you believed.

˜Spring˜

Rebirth
Renewal
Love, Hope, and Growth

Cookie's Jar

ookie was my older sister, and I loved watching her every move. Cookie was taller than me and slim. Her shoulder-length hair had a hint of golden-brown strands that danced along with her big brown eyes. We were a year apart, and we were the best when we were at our best. I loved her like no other and often wondered if she loved me just as much as I loved her. People at our school teased us because of our names, Cookie and Candy. Crazy, right? That a mother would even consider such names. But there they were on our birth certificates, as if we were items from a corner store. Momma's justification for this foolery was that she wanted "twins." But we weren't born at the same time, so why Cookie and dangone Candy? Pick another name, already, like Angela or Sabrina—anything but this!

When Momma conceived us, she was on that stuff. I didn't know exactly what stuff, but she was on something. Momma finally got herself together. She discovered that things did not go the way that she'd dreamed or thought that they would; they only got worse as we got older.

Cookie always had this quietness about her. To me, she was the prettiest, smartest girl I know. At times, she didn't think of herself that way. But I loved her so much that I was always there to lift her up. I reminded her that things may be rough at home, but once we got older, we did not have to be products of our past.

Cookie had the best boyfriends too. They all seemed to be nice, cute, and had good jobs and futures. But for some reason, they didn't stay. All her girlfriends came and went too. With our being as close as we were in age, you'd have thought that I knew more. But she was good at concealing and hiding stuff. She said that she liked to keep to herself and focus. Focus on what? Instead of calling her Cookie, I began to refer to her as "Kooky" because she had started acting weird and doing what I thought were dumb or stupid things.

After high school, Cookie went off to school in Florida, and she came back a different person. That shy, quiet girl turned into someone else. Cookie acquired a taste for dressing differently, and I really liked it. Instead of dressing...hmm...what I considered as "homely," she turned it up a few notches to classy and sophisticated. But she could not get a job. Who would hire someone named Cookie?

As for me, I stayed home to attend community college and help take care of Momma. Years of drinking, drugs, and partying had taken a toll on her body and mind but not on her spirit. Momma had joined the neighborhood church and found God.

I was extremely happy that she was turning her life around. Most of her time was spent at the church and doing outreach for the community. Momma didn't look as she once had. She started to gray, and that once-cute figure was now only skin and bones. Every morning, I watched her perform her ritual of health and wellness, choking down a handful of vitamins, herbal supplements, and Ensure to aid in gaining some weight. She would spend hours praying and reading the Bible. Then off to church she would go.

I worked in retail at the mall. It wasn't what I wanted to do, but someone had to stay home and help. I was fortunate enough to get a car last summer, and I was very happy. No riding the bus anymore for me! The monies that I had "come into" were from my savings. Each summer, during the breaks, I would work two jobs and just put that money away for a rainy day. Fortunately, because everyone knew me, I would be hired. On my job applications, I would be very creative. Instead of writing my name as "Candy," I would put C., my middle name Marie, and my last name. This was the method I used until I felt ready to change my name. Plus, I didn't want to pay two hundred dollars to do so until I decided what that name would be. I urged Cookie many times to consider changing her name, but she didn't feel that it was necessary because she really wasn't looking for a real job.

Cookie had moved back home, and Momma's attitude had changed. At times, she did not seem to want her there. I observed that Cookie sensed this and could not figure out why the sudden change. She wondered if Momma had felt that way about her all along. Things between them got so tense that Momma started calling her the "devil's spawn," and I knew that this hurt Cookie. Instead of opening and talking about the things that hurt her, she resorted to social media. She posted messages that were ambiguous or clichés. At times, you would have to read between the lines to get her meaning. I hated this: Cookie lived in the same house, and we were family, but she chose to post her feelings in front of a world of strangers.

One day, Cookie didn't take too kindly to Momma's outbursts and lashes. She approached Momma and started what I remember as one of the biggest fights ever between them. "Momma, since I am the devil's spawn, who in the hell is my daddy? Who is the devil? Or is the devil you?" Cookie asked.

I watched Momma's reaction. She just went into her room and held her Bible.

Cookie stormed after her and screamed at her again. "Momma, who is he? Why don't Candy and I know who our father is? Why haven't we seen a man, a father figure, around here? Why?"

"Girl, if you don't lower your voice and stop talking to me with that tone, there's going to be some problems. This is something I am not about to get into with you. I won't. You hear me? It's not—it won't change anything! So you can just get out of my face with this old stuff, you hear me? Just leave it alone!" Momma screamed.

Cookie stormed out the door with a duffel bag of clothes. I watched Momma turn back to her room, her bony hands clenched around her crumbly, black Bible. She closed her door, and that was the last time I saw my momma's face. Just like that, she was gone.

After I buried Momma, I changed my name. It was time for me to move forward. I had not heard from Cookie, and no one else had either. I decided to go back to school and earn my master's degree in education so that I could give back to children in need. One thing that I observed from Momma while she was alive was giving back. She worked tirelessly in community outreach programs, feeding and helping others. As for me, not only was I in the school system, but I volunteered any extra time at the local center downtown, counseling and mentoring young girls. I thought this would be ideal. I would try to change one little girl's direction and path, one girl at a time.

I was the last one to lock up one evening, and a woman approached me. She was torn, battered, dirty, and had a stench about her. "Candy, is that you?" she said.

I stopped to look at her closely. It was Cookie! I hugged her despite her appearance. This was my sister, and I would do anything to have her back. "Where have you been, Cookie? Why have you been gone so long? You know that Momma—"

Cookie cut me off. "Yes, I know. Well, I heard, and I wanted to come back, but I couldn't. Candy, I found out some horrible things about us and our missing father, dad, or whatever you want to call him. I found out something about me too. I couldn't deal with any of the information. So here I am, a product of what I did not want to become: an addict, a bum, a nobody. In this bag is a journal, Candy. I journaled my thoughts every day. I want you to keep it."

"Wait, Cookie. Why are you giving me this? Come on. Get in the car and let me take you to my house and get you cleaned up. Would you be OK with that?" I wiped her face with a tissue.

Cookie nodded her head, got into the car, and immediately fell asleep. When we arrived, I helped her into my home. She had the same duffel bag she had stormed out of Momma's house with that day. I gave her a towel and washcloth to clean herself with. I warmed up some soup and made some tea, hoping we could catch up. But Cookie stumbled onto my couch, tired. She appeared to be thankful to be warm and safe. I covered my sister with a blanket and felt relief to finally have her back.

I went into her bag and pulled out the book in which she'd written all her hurts and fears. I settled in the chair next to her, covered myself with a blanket, and wept while reading the pages. I cried myself to sleep.

I woke up the next morning to find that Cookie had left, once again. This time, I knew I probably would not see her again based on the contents of her journal. My sister had a bipolar disorder and suffered from manic depression. Not facing these demons, she lived a life of disorder and eventually drowned herself in addiction, the same as Momma. The following spring, I got a call to identify someone who was possibly my sister. She had been taken to the nearest hospital and died of an overdose.

I was sad before that call. I was sad when we were kids and played together. I knew back then that something wasn't right about her, and there was no one my sister or I could turn to. But I was now at peace. She had given me her journal, which I would hold on to for the rest of my life. On the closing page, she had drawn hearts and written:

> *In Cookie's jar, you will find only Candy, because I*
> *love Candy the MOST.*

I cried as I reread the pages. I'd always loved my sister, and now I knew she'd loved me too.

Something New, Something Blue

*I*n traditional wedding ceremonies by rite, the bride was expected to have something new, which symbolized optimism; something blue, which stood for purity and love; and something borrowed, which symbolized borrowed happiness. I never dreamed that *borrowed* would go so far.

For me, getting married again seemed to be a million light-years away. I wanted a love every day, a Saint Valentine to fill my heart's desire. There were times I wanted to be out of this marriage. I was young and ambitious. He was older and looking for a wife who would stay home and not have a dream. It didn't feel right, and if there was a next time, I would do it the right way.

Meeting Kedrick just seemed so perfect. He would always brighten my days with the brightest mornings. Never did he miss calling me or sending a text to ask me how was I or for me to have a good day. His daily greetings were enhanced with the sexiest smile when I would see him, and never did he forget to compliment me from head to toe. He was too thoughtful, while my husband was rarely so. In fact, my husband didn't talk to me. Sometimes it seemed I was invisible to my husband.

I took Kedrick's advances in stride because I wanted to allow my heart to mend from this man, whom I considered to be my husband. I hurt constantly, and my husband knew this. Kedrick just felt right. My family felt that my husband was perfect—you know, established, stable, and a great provider. All of these things were pluses, but paying attention to me was where he failed. We tried all sorts of things to make the marriage work. We attended counseling, you name it. He would conform for a few weeks, then go back to the way he was. I couldn't conceive a baby as quickly as he wanted me to. The doctors said that it was due to stress and that I was trying too hard. If I relaxed, it would come naturally, they assured. I couldn't relax because sex was now a chore. I knew my husband loved me, but I felt so burned out. After all, the look in his eyes wasn't the same as Kedrick's. I was at the point of comparing the two men, and I was ready to see if the grass was indeed greener on the other side. During this ordeal, Kedrick was there, you know, as a friend. He'd be an ear that listened to me complain and wallow in my distress. It was different talking to him than to a girlfriend because he would listen and offer a male perspective. He would give me advice on how to handle my husband and how to become more sensitive to his needs. After a while, the counseling and the advice got old, and I became disinterested.

One day, Kedrick asked if I would like to join him and some of his coworkers for happy hour. I never hung out with anyone after work; that was not my thing. Besides, it felt like fraternizing, as I am one of the directors of the department. Mixing with others was a no-no in my book. But he worked for another company in the complex. I thought, What the heck. I have nothing to lose. I'd joined them for a few drinks, and then I would head home.

We had a great time. Kedrick told me to relax; this was just like networking, getting to know others in the professional corporate setting. And just like that, after some drinks and laughter, I was headed for home.

The next day, I saw Kedrick. I waved, but he seemed somewhat distant. "Hey, Kedrick. Is everything OK?" I asked.

He mumbled something vaguely and hurried across the yard. I shrugged and kept moving. I glanced at my phone; there was a text from my husband wishing me a great day and saying that he loved me. I responded with an emoji blowing a kiss and entered my building.

As I sat at my desk, it began to bother me that Kedrick had seemed distant. That was a first, and I sat there rewinding the evening to see if the drinks had made me do or say something inappropriate. Everything seemed to be OK, so I decided to message him. No response. I could see the typing movement but nothing. No words; just nothing. I sent another message: *I hope everything is OK.*

Finally, he sent a thumbs-up.

I wasn't sure what that meant. But for now, I would no longer pry or try to figure this young man out. I finished up my day and headed home.

The next day, Kedrick greeted me with a bright smile. "Good morning, sunshine. How is your morning so far?"

I wanted to be childish and ask him whom he was talking to because he was like Dr. Jekyll and Mr. Hyde between yesterday and today. I hesitated before I spoke; in fact, I didn't want to speak. A nice evening with the hubby, and here this fool comes. "I'm awesome, Mr. Kedrick," I said. "What's up with you?"

He laughed and then proceeded to offer a compliment. "You look nice today, as always. Hey, my apologies regarding the abruptness yesterday. It was a bad day, no fault of yours. I didn't want to be a bore with my silly antics. What are your plans for lunch today? Can we grab a bite?"

As badly I as I wanted to say no, I agreed to his advances. It was just a simple lunch. "Sure, we can do that. I have a few meetings. Do you mind if we hook up somewhere? Just let me know where."

"Aw, Ms. Lady, I wanted to pick you up, like a date. I'm just kidding. Sure. We can meet," he said. "How about the salad bar on Fifth? Is that OK? And what time?"

"How about we exchange phone numbers just in case my meetings run over?"

We bumped phones, and I walked on. I felt like Gloria in *Waiting to Exhale* as Marvin watched her walk away. And lo and behold, as I turned around, he was still standing there, smile and all, watching. This man made me feel like a teenager with a crush. This crush was refreshing and new. He felt like my Valentine!

We met for lunch that day and, from that point on, every single day. Lunches went from early breakfast to dinner and sometimes dessert. Kendrick was willing to spend time with me, and I enjoyed every moment of it too. Our meetings eventually became intimate, with hugs and gentle kisses that would warm my entire soul. To finish off, I would go home and make love to my husband, and of course, he would have no complaints.

About three o'clock one morning, my phone went off. It was a text from Kedrick. He asked me what I was doing. What? Should I text him back? I decided not to. I turned my phone off and decided to deal with him in the morning.

On my way into work, Kedrick called. "Hey, Ms. Lady. I've been thinking about you all night, as you can see. I thought about you so much that I had to call you and ask if I could steal a few hours from you."

"A few hours? What do you mean?" I asked.

"I just want to see you. That's all. Can you meet me at Piedmont Park, the side where the lake is?"

"Sure, I guess." I emphatically did not deny his request. In fact, I drove fast and sent an email to my team saying that something had come up and that I would be in later. As I pulled up, there he was, waiting, parked by a tree. He gestured for me to join him in his truck.

As I got in, he grabbed me around my neck and started unbuttoning my blouse. He kissed me warmly and gently over each breast, making his way down to my hardened nipples. He came back up and softly kissed my dripping lips and pulled my skirt up. He gently stroked my thighs until he made his way to my love nest. I couldn't believe what I was allowing him to do to me. I didn't stop him. Somehow, he pushed the seats as far back as they would go and made his way over to my side. He pulled my thong over to the side and kissed each side of my thighs until he touched me with his tongue, and just like that, I was gone. I pushed his head for more and more while his hands fondled my breast. I was so gone again. He came up and kissed me and coyly said, "I wanted to taste you all night long, and I wanted to bless you today. Do you feel blessed?"

I was without words.

He then said, "By the way you're trembling, I'll take that as a yes." He kissed my forehead, and I tried to get myself together because that was totally unexpected.

My phone rang, and it was my husband. That got my mind straight. Kedrick reached over and opened the door for me. I exited his truck, and he waved good-bye.

All day, I couldn't focus. I canceled my meetings and kept my door closed. What the hell happened? A text appeared, and it read: *I am going to do things that will make you feel appreciated and wanted. With me, you will never have to worry ever again if you are loved.*

All I could do was exhale. This guy was in my head, and now there was no turning back, at least not yet. A few weeks went by like this. Sexcapades in the park at dark, for lunch, for breakfast, you name it. I even went as far as inviting him to come to my building, and that night, I went for it. Kedrick had me on the wall, on my desk, on the floor. Repeatedly, I would come to where I couldn't do anything but cry. He kissed the tears from my face and said to me softly, "I know."

I was done again and again.

It was now getting harder for me to go home and face my *husband*. He would be so excited to see me, and I would shower and throw my ass on him as quickly as possible to shut him down. Guilt was now tearing me apart. I'd gone so far with Kedrick. Not only that, I was losing myself professionally. I picked up my phone and texted him:

> *Hey, we need to talk. See you in the morning at the*
> *coffee shop.*

I thought, tomorrow morning when I am to meet him, I would end this escapade or at least slow it down.

We met as agreed, but the conversation didn't go as planned. He was angry. I was surprised that he was angry, but we didn't have a title on us anyway. Little did I know. Kedrick flipped the conversation and said that the ultimatum would be for me to leave my husband and be with him or we could never speak to each other again.

What bothered me about him was that I didn't know much about him, but I was so gone that I was willing to do it. Marriage between the husband and me was boring. Kedrick was spontaneous. Everything about him kept me wondering and longing, always wanting more.

Somehow, I separated from my husband so that I could give Kedrick and me a try. Foolish, right? However, I was young, and I needed more. I had never been loved like that. I didn't have to wait for stupid Valentine's Day to be loved every day the way I wanted to be. Each day, we would go home or to the place that I made home, and it would be an adventure. We went for long walks, found trees, and made love where we wanted to. I was always on ready, and he wanted me.

One day, I wanted to surprise Kedrick with a gift. We hardly ever spent the night together and woke up in each other's arms. He said that his company was installing a new server, and it required that he work at night. That morning, I waited and waited and no Kedrick. I dialed and texted and got no return call or text. I got worried because we were several months strong in this relationship, and there had been no drama. The gifts I had for Kedrick were my divorce papers and a pregnancy stick—POSITIVE! I was finally free, and I really could have a baby.

My divorce would be quick and easy—no kids or property that I was willing to fight over. Hell, he could have it all with his boring ass. We couldn't conceive together. Therefore, it had to be him and not me. I finally felt like I had my "something new," my optimism for a new future with someone who made me feel whole. I could be his, and he, mine.

About 2:00 a.m., Kedrick made his way in.

"Hey, baby, where have you been?" I said. "I've been trying to reach you the entire night."

Kedrick threw his keys on the counter and carried me to the sofa. "Baby," he said, "we need to talk."

Oh shite, I thought. My heart was pounding a thousand beats per minute. In fact, I thought I was going to pass out from not knowing what to expect from his response.

"This is so hard, but we never talked about this," he said.

I waited for a minute and wanted to show him my gift. Just maybe, he would be excited about it. I knew, too, that he was having issues at work. I quickly pulled the stick from behind my back. I was so excited. I had on one of his work shirts; I was tired but trying to maintain my sexy. "Dadeee, we're having a baby!" I jumped up and rushed around the counter. I flipped the paper over. "Look, baby, the divorce papers. We talked about this almost every day. Just like you wanted."

"We can't do this. I have to go back home—to my girl."

"What in the hell do you mean 'your girl'?" I demanded.

He stood up. "Look. You never asked. You never asked when I would leave, where I was going, or where I had been. I figured that us getting this spot together would save on the expense of hotels and prevent us from getting a ticket for lewd behavior in the parks and wherever else we had sex. Look, I got caught up, and so did you. Things moved too fast. I mean, how far are you with this pregnancy anyway?"

My heart was beating so fast that I was afraid to respond. "I'm early, maybe two months. It's just the mere fact that I could conceive—"

Kedrick interrupted me. "Yeah, I know. I know. You thought you couldn't have a baby. And you damn sure can't have this one either. At least not by me! I can't go through this with you. And I am sorry that you filed. That's something I didn't take seriously. I didn't think you would do that. You kept saying you still loved your husband. I belong to—"

I stood up, went across the room, and got in his face. "Son of a bitch, are you for *real*? Are you *serious*? *Am I really hearing this shite that you are saying to me?*"

Shots rang out.

Dear Momma,

I am doing fine, and I am getting along as best as I can with everyone. Thank you for sending me pictures of Kayla. She has gotten so big. The DA said that Kedrick is still on life support. If he dies, my sentence may be longer. I don't care, Momma. I should've been a little smarter by asking questions. I think about my vows to my husband every day and you and my sisters making a fuss to be sure that I had my "something new, something blue, something old," and I didn't realize that I would also get some-thing "borrowed": a fool who belonged to someone else. And now, I am literally on borrowed time.

Take care of Kayla, and I love you. Until next time.

Ode to Poppa

I couldn't believe Sharay dropped that BS on me! The first time she told me that she was pregnant, I went along with it, and now, less than a year later, another baby. I love Sharay, but enough is enough.

Me, I'm going to take care of my responsibilities. I mean, I played along with her, so I have to be responsible for my actions. I told her, though, that I did not want any children—at least not by her. Things were really good with us before she had the girls.

Sometimes, though, living with Sharay was difficult. I mean, she was moody.

I remember one time she invited me over for a cookout. When I would go by her parents' house to visit, I thought there was a hidden camera filming them. We all have some dysfunctional family members, but Sharay's family was the cream of the crop.

The weather was perfect for the cookout. Sharay's father asked me to help put out lawn chairs and tables. Any time a girl's father treats you like family, it's always a good thing. This Memorial Day gathering would be a big event. We cleaned about fifty chairs and ten tables. Sharay and I covered all the tables, smiling and gazing into each other's eyes. We dressed alike that day. I purchased our outfits. We both had on jean shorts and white polo shirts. We even went as far to wear the same shoes, white K Swiss. I also bought us matching floating-heart necklaces. She wore the left heart and I wore the right. We were a true couple.

Sharay's father tossed a wet towel to me. "Son, be sure to wipe the tops of the tables before you two put the cloths on the tables. I surely appreciate you coming over early to help."

Sharay smiled and hugged her father. "Oh, Dad, you know we didn't mind coming over to help. Besides, that crazy brother of mine is probably nowhere to be found. So, Dad, we don't mind." I loved being a part of her family—before that dreadful day took place.

Around four o'clock, crowds of people started flowing in from every direction in the neighborhood. Some of the family members had food items, drinks, and Tupperware containers for any leftovers they would take back home with them. The music was on point. Sharay's uncle, "Uncle Junior," as the family called him, was the DJ for the evening. Everybody's party always included Maze's song, "Before I Let Go." Sharay's mom came out and got people on their feet, and of course, we all had to do the festive line dance. After a few rounds of dancing, it was chow time.

Sharay's father asked us all to bow our heads so that he could bless the food. I wasn't sure if Sharay's brother heard his dad say anything about praying—perhaps it was due to the earplugs that he had on while talking on the phone. All of a sudden, Sharay's father sprinted across the yard, snatched the phone out of her brother's hand, took the earplugs, and stomped them to pieces. I couldn't believe her father fought his own son as if he were some dude off the street. If everyone wasn't startled, I was. I looked at Sharay, but she dismissed it as if it never happened.

Soon after that debacle, we prayed, we all sat down, and everyone started to pass different dishes across the tables. Sharay's mom looked disturbed and kept staring at Sharay's father as he fixed his plate.

"Why are you fixing your plate?" she asked. "You know that I fix your plate. Why are you fixing your plate?" These questions went on for a good ten minutes, which eventually led to a big argument and then to another fight. Food went flying everywhere. I couldn't believe something so simple had escalated to a fight—and most of all, in front of everyone. While all of this was happening, Sharay just sat there. I grabbed her as beans and ribs splattered on her white polo shirt, and we ran out and never looked back.

Fast forward. Our fights would be similar. Sharay would get disgusted with me about the most minor things. To calm her, because I loved her, I would hug her and tell her that it was my fault. Everything became my fault. One day, when I came home from work, Sharay was sitting in our living room, smoking a joint and snorting powder. In disbelief, I knocked the pot from her hands. Yep, I sure did. No woman of mine will ever use drugs, although I've used them a time or two.

As time went by, we eventually got back to "normal." When Sharay told me that she was pregnant with Cookie, I was happy. I didn't like the fact that she wanted to name the po' chile Cookie, but anything for Sharay. Cookie was the apple of my eye. She had a head full of hair, she was chubby, and she had large brown eyes. As Cookie grew older, she started acting strange. I noticed that the girl wouldn't talk, and at times, she wouldn't look at anyone. I told Sharay that we needed to get the girl checked out, but she didn't think anything was wrong.

Eventually, Sharay acted as though she didn't like Cookie. She was so frustrated with her that she thought it would be best to have another kid.

Another one? We were barely making ends meet with this baby. Sharay later announced that she was pregnant again.

Me, I had to ask how in the hell did this happen?

Sharay was so angry with me that she told her family everything—making me look like the bad guy. I should've stopped while I had the chance, but I loved Sharay, and I only wanted the best for her and the babies. She blamed me for everything. I guess it was because I allowed it. She eventually told me to get out.

I did not want any dealings with her and her family. She didn't want me at the house. She no longer allowed me to be a father to our daughters. She included her family in matters they shouldn't have been involved in. So I left, just like that.

All the doctors in the room looked at one another. The one closest to the patient closed her notebook and said, "Interesting story, Mr. Smith. Do you know how long you've been here at

Bellevue Psychiatric? You've been in and out since your second daughter, Candy, was born. Do you remember that? You were an outpatient at the time. Therefore, the times that you recalled leaving Sharay and your children were the times you checked in or out of this facility. Many times, we've told you that you suffer from dissociative identity disorder."

"What do you mean?" Smith asked.

The therapist said, "You have multiple personalities. Somehow, you have crossed things that happened in your past and made them Sharay's life. We are so sorry that you suffered trauma as a child because of your parents. Sharay tried to do what she could, but she battled her own demons too."

Smith looked down at his hands. "Well, how did I get here? And how long have I been crazy?"

"You're not crazy. You need help in sorting the past and present. Like most patients like yourself, you have some symptoms of false memory syndrome. You were committed as inpatient after heavy drug use, which only escalated your issues. Luckily, the mother of your children did not use them as frequently as you did, and she eventually went cold turkey. After years of hope that you would recover, we learned that one of your kids was afflicted with the same symptoms as you."

Smith began to get excited. "Now, now, Sharay had issues too. I mean, she would do things that didn't make sense. So my child Cookie couldn't be sick in the head because of me."

The second clinician slowly responded, "Yes, Sharay suffered from bipolar depression. But the times she acted 'differently' were because she didn't take her meds as prescribed.

But look, we are here to continue to help you. We just want you to get the facts straight and differentiate your past life and Sharay's. Understand?"

Smith stood up and walked to the barred window. "So the cookout, the time her father, I mean, my father…the person on the phone…the fight. No, no, that was her brother. It was me? My dad…Oh God! I repeated things my dad did to my mom… Oh God, to Sharay?"

The clinician stood and walked toward Smith. "Yes, it seems that this is true. Based on past notes from our team and the meetings we had with Sharay and your mother, you don't have a brother. That incident at the cookout was the final trigger. You attempted to move on with your life, but things only progressed. Unfortunately, your daughter Cookie dealt with her agonizing thoughts and behavior with drugs that only got the best of her. You can get better and perhaps, maybe, just maybe, spend some time with your daughters, especially, Candy. We're not sure how much longer you will continue to be here. However, you can write or call and see if they're willing to visit so you can sort things out with them. You can get started today. We have a number for you to try. Should we try?"

Smith took the phone. While the clinician dialed the number, he exhaled and listened for the voice on the other end. "Hello? Hello, Candy, it's me, Daddy."

~Summer~

Some of y'all walk around angry all the time
because you never learned how to forgive people.
The bitterness you're walking around with only
holds you back. Meanwhile...the people that
wronged you are somewhere not worried about you.
Don't let the actions of another keep you from
being happy.

~Blair Nash, Author & Relationship Strategist

Enemy with a Hidden Face

I loved hard and worked hard. I'd been married to my lovely wife for ten years, and Mia had proved her worth to me as a great woman and mother to my kids. We met in college. I saw her walking the yard and thought she was the most beautiful girl I ever laid eyes on. I remembered how she'd always held her books close to her. How fast she walked, looking straight ahead and hardly talking to anyone. There may have been two or three friends with whom she'd hung out on campus but never a large crowd. She dressed so-so and was the least fashionable. She never watched the Greeks as they walked through the campus; she modeled the type, but she demonstrated no interest.

I must say something to my future queen, I thought. She intrigued me from afar. One sunny afternoon, I decided to catch up with her, and just like that, she smiled and gave me the best opportunity of my life.

Mia was not easy either. Because I played sports and was privileged with a nice car, being with other women was effortless. Our conversation came with ease but not the panties. This was cool. Finally, a challenge. That sunny Friday afternoon, "hello" went on for several hours, into the wee morning hours. After talking with her all night about anything and everything, yes, I decided she would be the one.

I proposed to Mia our senior year in undergrad. Mia thought seeking a master's degree would be valuable, so I enrolled in graduate school. We graduated at the same time but ended up attending different schools in different states, me out west and Mia up north.

We talked several times a day. We would often FaceTime or Skype with each other. We made time for each other and kept our relationship spicy and interesting. During our time away from each other, I made sure I kept my nose clean. Being faithful to Mia was at the top of the list. After our first year in grad school, we received blessings from both of our parents and got married. Our wedding was everything to us. What was most important to me was that she got the wedding that she wanted. Mia was there for me and faithful. I trusted her with my life. I trusted her with my soul. For the remainder of grad school, we lived somewhat awkwardly in separate spaces. However, we made it work.

Mia could cook, and lovemaking with my Mia was heaven. Sometimes I believed that it was mainly due to missing each other and because our contacts were few and far between. It was not like the others. Being with her reminded me of my first time. Yes, a virgin all over again. She knew every part of my body and what turned me on. I remembered one night she kissed me in places she'd never traveled to before. There were two voices speaking to me: one said to enjoy it, and the other wondered if she had experimented with someone else. Why were men so crazy? Why was it that if we didn't pull the rabbit out of the hat, it had to have been someone else? Insecurity was nothing but fear, but that night, it showed up in our bed. The greatest weakness for us men was our ego.

Once we finished school, we were both blessed to land great jobs. We built our lives next, buying a home and immediately starting a family. When we gave birth to our son—I remembered like it was just yesterday—I felt like the luckiest man in the world. We named him Nolan Bryce—Nolan after my brother and Bryce for one of her siblings. Taking her and Nolan home, I knew that the magic would continue. I offered them my very best and then some.

As the years grew on us, sometimes it felt like life itself was turning but not downward. We took family trips in between work and made our family the priority. Sometimes life was too good. So good it was almost boring. I had the world in my hands. There were no money woes. We rarely argued. However, it was boring. I needed some action in my life. Because I played ball in college, I joined this recreational team to bounce in between Nolan's soccer and T-ball games. I coached his T-ball games whenever I did not have to travel for work.

Mia's parents had come into town, and this allowed us some free time with a sitter. I took Mia to the mountains so that we could have some us time and wind down from the daily riff. We did some wine tasting, climbing, boating; you name it, we did it. We had a fabulous time, and we didn't want to go home.

It was back to work and my routine basketball games at the rec center. The center was becoming more popular and drawing different crowds. The center added exercise equipment and classes, such as yoga and Spinning. One night, Mia called to inform me that she hadn't cooked and that I should grab a bite to eat. For some reason, I didn't want to go home and feel trapped and closed. I went to the locker room, showered, and then headed over to the local bar and grill, which remained open until midnight. I sat at the bar to eat and watch ESPN.

This broad came in and sat down next to me at the bar. She was breathtaking in beauty. She seemed to have some "sport smarts" too. Body, eh, so-so. A smile good enough to appear in a commercial. For a quick second, I got lost. However, I was quickly reminded of my marriage by the diamonds embedded in platinum. They glistened softly under the low bar lights, saying, "Go home, Kevin."

Her name was Keima. Wow. Keima…I found myself not wanting to go home. She handed me a business card. Ms. Keima was into real estate. I took her card. I shook her hand and told Keima good night. On my drive home, the only thing I could think about was feeling free and having a refreshing conversation. Yeah, it was nothing like kicking it with the boys and talking a lot of nonsense. The opposite sex was different— even more so when it was not your wife.

~Not Ready~

Mia called me today at work with the most distracting news: another baby. I wasn't ready for a new baby. I was just promoted within my company; I had finally made it to VP. With my new position and income, Mia was taking time off work to raise Nolan. We talked about having more kids, but we also said that we would wait. This frustrated me. Who was to blame? Me? I required sex often. Therefore, if I was the one who was not ready, then maybe I should have jimmied it up. I swung around in my chair, pouting. I'll just bury myself in work, I thought. I told Mia, "Don't wait up for me."

I left and went to the local bar and grill, and guess who was there? Keima. Yes, Ms. Keima was dressed up with a suit and briefcase. She sat at one of the tables in the bar area with a person who presumably was a client. There was an exchange of paperwork across the table. I sat down at the bar, periodically turning my head to be sure that she was still there and had not left without gracing me with her beauty and presence. I ordered a few drinks and tapas, waiting patiently. Keima finished up and came over with a walk that I didn't realize the first night. I saw her. Whatever. I needed someone to talk to because I needed to let off some steam.

We talked and talked. Eventually, we moved from the bar to a table. For some reason, I wanted a table that was somewhat intimate. As I walked Keima over to the table, I quickly removed my ring from my finger. I wanted no reminders that night.

We agreed to leave, and next thing I knew, I was following Keima to her spot. My heartbeats were irregular. I told myself that I had self-control. I would not go any further. I honored and respected my union, and I would not disrespect Keima. We arrived at her spot, which was not far from the bar and grill. She led us to the deck, which overlooked the city. Keima poured us both water and a glass of Pinot Noir.

"Hey, Kevin, do you mind if I change? I've been in this suit all day. These CLs are killing me."

I coyly responded, "Yeah, sure. It's your spot, and I am only a guest."

Keima came back in this nice flowered dress and slides. I surely hope she doesn't make it easy for me, I thought. "What are you thinking, K?"

I mumbled.

"Kevin, did you say something?" Keima asked.

"No, no. Just thinking out loud. Silly me. Nice place you have here. You have an awesome view too."

"Thank you. I bought this place as a steal, especially since I work in real estate."

Everything began to fast forward. Keima walked over to my chair and sat on my lap. While straddling me, she unzipped my pants and pulled on me. She went down right away. I couldn't believe one, she was doing this, and two, I didn't stop her. Once she worked up a wood, she opened a magnum, and I was inside her. I held on to her buttocks as she ground me slowly and sultrily. She kissed my neck, my shoulders, and went to work on me. We finished together.

Once my breathing caught up with my heartbeat, she looked into my eyes and said, "I am not a home wrecker. This is for me. I want you, and you want me. I have no expectations from you. Ever. Understand?"

I did not know how to respond. Before I could answer, she slowly started biting on my bottom lip, replaced the magnum with another, and worked me over and over again.

I pulled into my driveway at 1:00 a.m. Shite! What had I done? What was I thinking about? No need to feel guilty, right? Do I call my dudes? Naw, naw, you can't do that. I unlocked the door and headed straight to the shower. While in the shower, I scrubbed my mustache, goatee, ears. Any and every part of my body that had touched Keima's body. I feared that Keima's honey might be in my tee, so I just shaved all the hair from my face. As I scrubbed my face, I could still remember what she tasted like. This was crazy. OK, OK. First time, last time. Dumb, maybe. However, women just seemed to know everything. No chances here. No f**kups. Not any additional ones, anyway.

After I put my things in the hamper to be laundered, I tip-toed to Nolan's room. He slept so peacefully. All sorts of guilt washed over me. I just wanted to hold him. I did something so stupid, I could lose it all. I got into the bed, and Mia snuggled up to me.

She whispered, "Sorry, baby, for the fight we had earlier. I should have protected us when I knew that a baby was not the right time. I am sorry."

For some reason, all I could do was hold Mia. I did not say a word. I just held her and prayed that daylight would come. I wanted this night to be over.

~House Calls~

I got up early. It was Saturday, and I was happy that the weekend was finally here. Keima and I had several night, morning, and afternoon events like the first night. I had a newfound addiction, and she was my drug. But this addiction was worse than any drug, and it went on for months. I became sloppy with my affair with Keima. We were seen everywhere and with everyone—except family. I had so much to lose, and my family was at the top of that list. I decided to back off for a while, as Ms. Keima stated emphatically each time I left her that she was not a home wrecker and that there were no expectations.

It had been some weeks since I'd talked to Keima, and I wanted it to remain that way. It was close to the delivery date for our new baby girl, and I needed to get my act together. The smells of sweet hickory bacon, pancakes, and scrambled eggs and cheese danced their way through the house. I went into the kitchen, and there was my family, Mia and Nolan happily entertaining each other. I kissed Mia on the forehead, picked up my baby boy, and tickled him a few times. "Nolan, you want to take a walk with Daddy to the mailbox?"

"Yes, Daddy. Wait for me. I have to put on my shoes."

I laughed. "Come on, run quick." I went out to the driveway for the newspaper and then to the mailbox. I flipped through the mail and noticed a flyer insert in the stash. "What the eff?" The flyer was from Commerce Realty with Keima S. Molloy, Realtor and broker. I became extremely angered and fearful at the same time. Mr. Roberts, my neighbor, was out doing yard work.

"Hey, Mr. Roberts, great day for planting, huh?" I fidgeted with the mail.

"Hi there, son. How is everything going? Oh, you have li'l man with you. Hi, li'l man, how is T-ball going? Any home runs?"

Nolan proceeded to answer. Before our neighbor could respond, I was eager to ask my question. "Mr. Roberts, um, has there been any talk about any sellers in the neighborhood?"

Mr. Roberts looked curious. "No, not that I know of. Why do you ask?"

I cleared my throat before I responded, "I just wondered if there was any talk in our neighborhood. I keep getting this junk mail from this Commerce Realty and wondered if anyone else was getting the same stuff in the mail."

Mr. Roberts replied, "No, we haven't received any junk mail from any realty companies. I can't say that we have."

I walked away from Mr. Roberts. "Nolan, tell Mr. Roberts good-bye." Nolan waved. I walked to the trash can and tossed the flyer away. Once I got back into the house, I did not have much of an appetite. I washed my hands, sat at the table, and slowly ingested a slice of bacon while thinking what my next move would be.

A few weeks had passed since the Keima's stunt of putting her info in my mailbox. I decided that if I contacted her and told her that I got it, she would continue with the nonsense. My fear was that this woman had come to my house. As hooked as I was on Keima, I had not disclosed to her where I lived. I knew, too, that it would not be rocket science for a Realtor to find out where I lived. However, I thought that Keima and I were hella cool and that she wouldn't do anything stupid like that. Our sexcapades had turned into something more.

~*New Arrivals*~

Baby Nicole was here. She was beautiful and juicy. I know that I wasn't accepting earlier, but a man's heart changed like the wind. Mia had to have a C-section because Nicole weighed in at nine pounds. I had taken a few weeks off from work to help Mia at home with the chores and see after Nolan. While Mia was home, she also took lead in relocating us in a bigger home. I had entrusted her with the task of finding the property; the cost of the new home was not an issue. Anything that involved real estate I wanted no part of. Some would've thought I was crazy and that it was risky to allow only my wife to be involved in such a big investment. I trusted Mia as my power of attorney, and she was intelligent enough to handle our financial affairs.

Unfortunately, I had to return to work. I did not want to leave my beautiful family, but bills had to get paid. Once I got back home, there were boxes everywhere. I decided to clear out some of the items while Nolan was at school. The movers had moved all the larger pieces of furniture and placed them in their respective rooms. Most importantly, I wanted all the bedrooms to be suitable so that my babies could come home and be comfortable. I had also hired some cleaning help. This would be good. A new start in life. A baby and home. No Keima. That part of my life was short-lived and over. I tried convincing myself that it had just been sex. That's all: sex.

It was much more, though. Sex all times during the day. Spending time, conversation, and so on. It would be a train wreck about to pop off. So I'd ended it. Besides, whatever we'd had was interrupting my clarity and how I looked at my Mia. Mia was my everything. My rock. Keima no longer reached out to me except for that stunt with her business card flyer in my mailbox. She had gotten my attention, and that told me to leave her ass alone. I was thankful for my new arrival and beginnings. She could move on with her life, and so would I.

~Keima S. Molloy~

OK, my momma didn't raise any fool, but there were times when I wasn't listening. I couldn't resist. When I first laid eyes on him, I thought, what a beautiful creation! The ring on his finger wasn't missed. I had never been with a married man. However, it did not seem to bother him, because we talked about everything. This was a sign to me that it wasn't all that at the house. So I became selfish. Oh wait, I am already selfish. But I had no expectations, and I am single. I never thought that it would go as far and as long as it did. I thought the one night he followed me home would be it. I got caught up. I didn't care. I never knew his last name. He gave it to me like he cared and then some. I enjoyed it, and so did he.

One thing that I was not about to do was become a stalker or someone who cried over a married man. I did not try hard enough, I guess. We made it work based on the time that we had between us. I knew within my heart that it was more than sex. I'd been with someone who was sex only. To help me get back my focus once he stopped answering my calls and text messages, I backed off too. I had to protect myself because it was only me. I did not do my due diligence in terms of how deep Kevin's relationship was with his wife. He never spoke badly about her. He needed me. I gave him intimacy. Companionship. Friendship.

~Mia~

Kevin becoming the VP in his company elevated his status and our bank account. I worked hard during grad school and continued to do so after I graduated. Building a family was something that I dreamed of, and I knew that doing this would be good for us. As I held Nicole, I felt complete. A boy and now a girl. I whispered to baby Nicole, "You are beautiful, intelligent, and strong. You're able to do all things and anything that your heart desires. No man or woman should ever break you. You are empowered to do great things."

Kevin empowered me to do all things. In fact, he didn't realize how much power he had given me. He often thought of me as simple. I bored him. I did not dress a certain way. I did not "turn tricks" for him in the bed a certain way.

One night, Kevin came home frustrated. I could tell. The fool shaved his mustache and tee. This was the night that I felt that Kevin had changed. He came in late. He started criticizing how and what I wore when previously it was never an issue. He required that my hairstyle change, when this man would wash my hair and practically lie in it. Yes, there had to be another woman. However, I had to play it cool.

When I told him that I was pregnant? He lost it. He left the house again as usually did after we fought, and he stayed gone all night as if it was my fault. I chalked it up. I apologized so that we could move forward. Then the lying, the later nights. Kevin became nervous. He no longer needed me for making love. It would be brief, and he would roll off and pretend to be fast asleep.

One day, I decided to investigate. Oh no, no private eye for me. Just wait for it. He didn't care anymore. He just allowed me to be responsible for signing everything. So I did. I signed everything in my name and waited until the day I could prove he was out being an idiot. Why my name? Because it would be mine, and he would have to start over with nothing. On countless nights, he left me feeling like nothing while taking care of Nolan and pregnant with his second child. Women are so stupid too. A married man rarely leaves his wife for another woman. Too much at stake.

It all came out with the move. Kevin wanted to move quickly, as if that would change things. I met Keima S. Molloy, highly recommended. I called her, and we agreed to meet. We agreed as client and agent. She led me to the other missing parts of the puzzle. So accommodating. The fragrance of the perfume. The recommendation of the hair salon to style my hair. Ms. Molloy's look would be my new look. The gifts, shoes, purses—all from Kevin. Extraordinarily coincidental, right? No.

One day, Kevin called while she was out with me, showing homes. Dumb broad had the audacity to have my Kevin's face with his contact number. She could do this. He could not. She talked to him briefly, and the heifer's total demeanor changed. Oh, for most women we recognize when there is a man present in another woman's life. Once she ended the call, she could barely focus. She even had the nerve to abruptly stop showing the home, stating that she had an emergency. This meant only one thing: Kevin would leave work too.

So I decided to stop by his office, and of course, the fool was not there. However, I had the opportunity to speak with the CEO of the company. He was thrilled to see me. We chatted in his office, and he shared with me how Kevin had grown and how Kevin's stock in the company would be enormous by the end of the quarter. Game changer—I would stay until the stock, promotion pay increase, and bonuses were solid. All I could think about was how comfortable baby Nicole, Nolan, and I would be in our new home financed by the world's stupidest and dumbest daddy-husband. I went home and signed into our bank account. Money transfers, expenses, you name it. All for some so-so coochie. I would continue to play it cool. And wait.

At the closing, Keima could not focus. And for some reason, Kevin opted not to be there. She seemed to be a little different from when I first met her. Before, Keima was all giddy and smiling. So, knowing intuitively, I said, "Keima, you don't seem like yourself today. Is everything OK? I figured that you would be somewhat excited for this closing. You should be excited—no pregnant woman to follow you around anymore and oh, the commission. It's been months, and I really appreciate you."

Keima did not respond. I knew it was over between those two. He was home more, and her personality was less inflated. I didn't need to do anything to her because she was doing it to herself—she was miserable. As for Kevin, once I got home from delivering baby Nicole, there was no way he would continue to remain in the house with me. I wanted him out. He was with Keima for six months, if not longer. A quick slip, my ass. For me, it was over. He had done it once, and he would do it again.

~*The Enemy*~

Kevin picked us up from the hospital happy, feeling deserving. He had Nolan with him. We got home, and he waited on us hand and foot. Day by day, I began to get my strength back. He did a good job moving everything into its proper place. By week five, I'd lost most, if not all, of my baby weight. I felt like myself again. Kevin had gone back to work, and things seemed to be in place.

I left the house to meet with an attorney. I was filing for divorce. And I would take the stock, bonuses, you name it. Yes, I was done. The papers would be delivered to Kevin's job within the next week. Delivered? Dirty, huh? Why would I hand something to him personally? No, he needed to feel humiliated like I felt. Of course, I expected a phone call from him. He was a non-confrontational individual. Never would he talk to me in person. However, I was ready.

That day, he came home early. He was frantic. He questioned what this was all about.

"It's about me and this family," I shouted. "Me being in the background while you were out making it happen. And by the way, I met your little girlfriend. You gave it all away when I put her flyer in the mailbox. You really thought she did that? If Keima had come near my home, I would've killed her!"

"That was you? You put that in the mailbox? But why?"

See, men are also slow. I threw Kevin off by bringing in something small and distracting. "Oooh, so you're admitting that you know this chick? And get this. I want a divorce, and I want you out! You humiliated me, wanting me to look like her! How dare you, Kevin. Then you would go out and screw her and then come home, shave your mustache and tee so that your chin wouldn't smell like ass? You nasty son of a b—"

"No, no! Are you crazy? Is this what this is about? It was only one time, Mia. I promise."

"Kevin, you are such a liar. That chick showed me this house! Did you know that? You called her while I was out with her. How do I know this? Smartphones with pictures on them—yours!"

Kevin paced the floor. "This is so stupid. You don't work. This new house?"

I felt confidant. "This new house is in my name. You elected *not* to show up for the signing, remember? And work? Who needs to? I spoke with your boss one day when you were out with this bitch. Your stocks and bonus? *Mine!* Pack your shite and get out, Kevin! Just go."

Kevin headed for the bedroom and put a few things into his LV overnight bag. Little did he know I'd ship his remaining items to Keima.

"Hello, Keima? Hey, girl, it's me, Kevin. I need a place to stay. Can we talk?"

I missed Kevin. No lie. I mean, I met this man while finding myself in college. He was like my first. Well, almost my first. He was the first man who loved me. For months, I cried, wondering what I did wrong or could have done better. I cooked, cleaned, and made love to my husband at the drop of the dime. I was not enough, and I was not good enough.

I went through torture for months after I found out who Kevin was out screwing around with. I compared my hair with hers and my body, my clothes, you name it. I found myself competing with a woman who loved my husband more than she loved herself. This woman knew about his children and me, but she knew nothing about our covenant, and she did not care.

Everything had to change for me. The church in which we worshipped became a place of whispers each time the kids and I would enter. Keima and Kevin would come as a "couple" to worship. We would try to avoid each other by attending different services. However, it seemed that everyone knew we were no longer Mr. and Mrs. Roberts. Their stares did not make it any better either. It did not make me uncomfortable with fear, but it compromised my integrity and character as a woman and mother. I often found myself wanting to ask boldly who the hell they were looking at. I felt the strong urge to tear someone's face or eyes with my good left hook. Oh yeah, the rumors were thick at church too. I could no longer get the word of God without hearing that Keima couldn't wait for Kevin to propose to her. She wanted to become his wife. They'd started a business together. They had to do something. Job security was null and void for Kevin. By the time I got his stupid tail for his bonuses and 401k, the company decided that it was in his best interest to resign. So he and Keima started a real estate business. I could take that too. But I was tired. It was time for me to stop dwelling in misery in the shadow of Kevin. If she wanted him, she could have him.

Our son missed Kevin dearly. That was understandable. However, Nicole did not know the difference. As far as she was concerned, I was both Mommy and Daddy. Kevin would come to pick up Nolan some weekends. Eventually, he became a deadbeat, stating that he had to work a lot to make ends meet. This greatly affected Nolan. I reacted quickly and asked that Kevin no longer come to get him and interrupt his life.

I found myself angry. Pissed. I had to do something. Again, I began to act out of character. Everything and anything emotional was all Kevin's fault. Slowly, I had become a victim. That was a badge that my girlfriends and I had vowed never to wear. Victim Queen. Victim and pitiful. On victim's row, she was accompanied by Angry Black Woman. I was angry about everything—the traffic light because it turned red, eggs because they had to be cracked if you want them scrambled. I was just *angry*. And, oh, poor me!

This attitude eventually distanced me from those who loved me. My friendships did not need adjusting—my closest friends took breaks from me. I had become so rigid and ugly that I decided to see a therapist. The "woe is me" had started affecting my relationship with my true heart—Nolan and Nicole.

~Getting Treatment and Treated~

My therapist was very nice and inviting. In fact, I could open up to him right away. After my sixth session with Dr. Chris, I got my confidence back. I was no longer a turtle in a shell that distanced herself from everyone. One thing that still disturbed me was Kevin not spending time with Nolan. Nolan missed his daddy very much. I couldn't take his daily questions regarding Kevin's whereabouts anymore.

One day, as I was leaving Dr. Chris's office, Kevin called. It was the worst argument between us ever. After our call ended, I slammed my phone against the wall, and it shattered into pieces. Dr. Chris ran out of his office, saying, "Mia, Mia, get up! Get up now. This is no time for setbacks. You're allowing yourself to no longer be *you*. We've worked hard to get back to this good place. Do not give up on you because of someone who obviously doesn't love himself. Remember what we discussed: misery loves misery, and hurt people only hurt others. Now get up and get yourself together."

I took the tissue that he offered without hesitation while trying not to make eye contact with him. I was embarrassed. I did not want to go backward. I knew that this was not going to be easy. I thanked Dr. Chris and hurried to the mobile store to purchase a new phone.

It was Friday, and I had no plans. One of my friends picked up the kids to give me a break. I logged on to my laptop and fooled around on the web for a few minutes. Boredom asserted itself, and I figured that there was no harm in setting up a profile for a dating web page and social media. "This should be fun," I said to myself. I answered some of the questions, gave myself the profile name "FLY-MOMMA," uploaded a picture, and I started receiving responses instantly. I got so good at social media that I learned how to upload photos of the places I was shopping, eating, or hanging out with the girls. This new life of mine was not too bad. In fact, I was learning things about myself and about things that I shouldn't have tolerated for so long.

Kevin no longer checked on the kids. He pretty much had given up on them both. Although no one could replace their father, I had a village of friends and family that support me with Nicole and Nolan.

After a few counseling sessions with Dr. Chris, I started to see him in a different way. It had been some years since Kevin and I had been intimate, and it appeared that I didn't have any options for soothing or comforting my body's withdrawal symptoms. I felt close enough to Dr. Chris, so I took a chance. As he talked about the opportunities that I should make in my life, everything he said sounded like the words of a broken, muffled robot. I did not want to hear him talk. I wanted Dr. Chris to fill me up and squeeze on every particle of my body. He peered over his glasses and notepad, and I decided to give him a seductive look to let him know that it was OK to come and get this. What was I thinking? I did not care. I wanted him. And besides, men were weak; I could make him want me.

"Ms. Roberts," he said, clearing his throat, "is everything OK?"

I nodded while refreshing my lip gloss. Dr. Chris adjusted his necktie, and he put his notepad down. I did not have to say anything. He knew I needed it. We talked about it in my sessions. Maybe we both took things too far? Maybe. Right then, I didn't care. I did not think he cared either.

Here he comes, I thought. His hands were all over me, squeezing me just the way I liked. Perhaps I set the stage with my sessions, telling him all my secrets that had been so bottled up and the things that I felt I needed. As he laid me down, every inch of my skin and body was being stroked and stimulated, reminding me of the beautiful woman that I was.

After my "session" with Dr. Chris, I stopped by my favorite restaurant to celebrate my singleness and the new freedom of being divorced and not having a care. I glanced over to the left side of the eatery and noticed Kevin at a table with someone. It wasn't Keima, though. I thought, I don't care. Yet something still consumed me. Out of boldness, I walked over to the table where Kevin and this mystery woman sat.

"Well, hello, Kevin."

Kevin looked startled. "Hi, Mia. I've been meaning to call you—"

I held up my hand to stop him from talking before he got started with some nonsense. "Whatever you say, Kevin, please just save—"

The woman stood up. "Hi, my name is Catherine. I've heard a lot about you. You must be Mia."

I looked at Kevin, wondering who this woman was who claimed to know me. "Where is your woman Keima? I can't believe you have not reached out to see your kids, Kevin. What about them? At least Nolan. You know what? I don't have time for this mess! I really don't! Just forget it! As a matter of fact, I am so angry right now. You know? Never damn mind!"

I stormed off. He had irritated me, and I allowed him to get under my skin. Again, I allowed someone who was not in my household to get the best of me. I went back to my table and pulled out my phone to write a post for social media: *Today was a good day and a bad day. Running into my ex shows that I have not passed the test. There are some people who deserve payback, and they don't deserve to enjoy the beauty of God's creation. I had to remind myself of the sensational man who reminded me how beautiful I am. Who cares if your ex has another woman? Taking the* high *road.*

Before I could put my phone away, I had more than fifty "likes," thirty-five hearts, and two mad emoticons. I enjoyed posting on social media. It was therapeutic. An inbox message appeared from Dr. Chris. Hmm, I thought, I didn't realize he was on Facebook. The message told me to be careful of what I post. *You never know who reads your information.*

I shrugged my shoulders and finished drinking my wine. The drive home was a pleasant one. I called my girlfriend to check in on the kids. She told me they were fine and to come by the next day to get them. Good thing it was summer and there was no school. I pulled into the driveway, regretting that

I did not leave any lights on. I hit my clicker for the alarm and the lights. Once I entered the house, I saw that it had been ransacked. I ran to the windows to see if there had been a forced entry. I was shaking badly when I tried to dial 911. The police arrived at my home quickly. Nothing had been taken. It was just someone in my things. I called my neighbors to ask if they had seen anything. The Kingsleys came over to make sure I was OK.

"Mia, we did see someone over here, but we thought that you were home," Mr. Kingsley said. "The woman who does the real estate for this side of town was here earlier. She waved and entered your home. We did not think anything of it. Sorry that we can't be of more help."

I was confused and angry at the same time. I could not believe Keima had the audacity to enter my home. How did she get the security code? I filed a report with the police and walked everyone to the door. As soon as I was alone, I got on the phone to Kevin to inform him that his hatchet woman had entered my home. I did not get an answer. I called Dr. Chris. No answer either. I ran upstairs to check my safe for my .38-caliber revolver. I mean, if she was so bold as to walk around in my home and go through my things, surely, she would return. If she decided to return, I would not have any issue about letting her know that she was trespassing. I knew that getting a good night's rest at home would be impossible. So I packed an overnight bag and headed to the Westin.

After a long soak in the garden tub and ordering room service, there was a tap on the door. I had invited Dr. Chris to complete my evening. I was excited about telling him what happened when I got home, and I longed for company for the night. We sat up and talked for the remainder of the evening. The light from the television flickered on the wall. A news ticker flashed on the television screen: "Real estate agent found slaughtered in Sanna Forest Estates."

I immediately sat up. "That's my neighborhood! What's going on now?" That idiot, Keima, had been in my home, and now this. Dr. Chris looked at me while rubbing my shoulders. "Do you want to call someone?" he asked. "The report did not state the address, but it's just odd, after your home was broken into."

Before I could thumb through my contacts on my phone, the phone rang.

"Hello, Mia? Where are you?" It was my neighbor. "Your home, well, a woman was found in your home, and the police and fire department are here."

"OK, Mrs. Kingsley. I am on my way."

Again, my phone rang with a call from an unknown phone number. "Hello, this is Mia."

"Hi, Mia," a man said. "This is Officer Daniels. How far away are you? We need you to identify the bodies—"

"Bodies? What do you mean *bodies*?"

Officer Daniels told me to get to my home right away. I rushed to put my clothes on and pack my things.

Dr. Chris grabbed me. "Hey, I think it would be good for me to go with you. You've been making progress in getting over that lying, cheating husband of yours. It was unfair, too, that a woman such as Keima would break covenants and not give a care about anyone but herself. Please, can I be there for you?"

My heart pounded. At last, someone seemed to care for me or about my well-being. I turned to Dr. Chris and took his hand. "Yes, please come with me. I don't understand why this is happening. Why my home? Here, please keep my gun on you while I gather my thoughts."

"Yes, Mia. I got you. I am here for you. Don't worry. I'm sure all of this will be sorted out once we get to your home."

~A New Enemy~

There was complete chaos in my driveway. Newscasters, police cars, and fire trucks were on every corner. I entered my home. There, on the kitchen floor, was a covered body, contorted as if it was attempting to run. Keima. She had been strangled and stabbed several times. Another body lay on the threshold of the back door, either coming in or leaving. When the detectives uncovered Kevin's body, I screamed. I was not prepared for that. It did not make sense.

The detectives led me into the living room and began asking me a gang of questions. The Kingsleys had come back over to console me. Dr. Chris had gone upstairs to gather some more clothing for me. There was no way I could stay in that house. I needed to get away and sort some things out. How would I explain Kevin's death to Nolan? It was bad enough that Kevin had not been there for his children.

Once the officers and the coroner departed with the deceased, I found some papers in another part of my home addressed to Kevin. In the envelope were pictures of Keima and a man. In some of the pictures, I noticed Keima, but the man was unidentifiable. Why wasn't this man Kevin? And who was the woman with Kevin at the restaurant? I thought that Keima was so in love with my husband and that she really had to have him. How did the detectives miss the envelope? I flipped through more pictures. One of the pictures was very familiar. I noticed the back of the man's head that looked like Dr. Chris. As I turned around, there was Dr. Chris, looking at me and then at the picture I held in my hand. Fear rushed over me. What was I to do next?

We stood there and stared at each other. Suddenly, I darted toward the door. Immediately, Dr. Chris came at me, blocking and shushing me while he moved his coat jacket to the side to show me that he had a gun. Frightened, I teared up, fearing his next move. I tried to run out of the house to get the attention of the officers before they pulled out of my driveway. Dr. Chris moved toward me again. All sorts of thoughts crossed my mind. What had I gotten myself into? I had to think quickly. Did he plan to do to me what he did to the others? No, this can't be true. No, he didn't do that. I trusted this man. He became my confidant when my stupid husband would not do right.

I could hear the officers' walkie-talkies. I could scream for help. Someone would be in here to look for me. That's it, and I could get away from this loony, messed-up-in-the-head man. I could hear my heart beating fast. When he moved his jacket again, I noticed that the gun was mine. I felt so stupid for entrusting him with my weapon at the hotel. He'd been in my house…Oh my! He tapped his fingers on my revolver. One of the officers reentered the house to leave his contact information. Dr. Chris moved to the corner, behind the door. I could read his lips: *If you say anything, I will kill you.*

Vee Jaye

I was tired of moving around. After my dad and mom divorced, it seemed as if no one wanted the responsibility for owning me. During the summer, every weekend, I had to pack up and go stay with my mother, my dad, and Big Momma too. I was restless that last summer, and I knew that the only way out was to stay busy as a summer camp counselor. That gave me some solace. Being around people who were somewhat strangers to me filled my heart and mind with positive thoughts.

At first, I wasn't sure how I should be feeling after they divorced. I didn't want to pick or choose, so I would hang out with both of them. I saw things that I didn't think a child should see. My dad had a mountain of girlfriends. Some would try to get into my good graces. They would gift me, feed me, or ask if I wanted to hang with them. The thing I hated the most was that when we left, these ladies would cry. I asked my dad why they were crying, and each time, his reply was that they were crazy. This stuck in my head forever. I took lots of notes, hanging out. Those notes eventually became my "what not to do" checklist.

When I hung out with my mom, the one crying was the opposite, but the response was similar. When we would leave her friends Larry or Jeff, she would cry. I asked her why. Her reply was that they were crazy, and they didn't know a good thang when they saw it. Yet she would frequently talk to them on the phone or visit them again—and she'd be crying and telling them the same thing.

By my fifteenth birthday, I needed a change. So I decided to give Big Momma, my grandmother, a chance. She had gotten older, and I knew she had slowed down on gambling and selling liquor from her house. But things weren't any different living with her. She had somewhat turned over a "new leaf" and had all sorts of walk to live with her. She said she was helping "others" by allowing these random people to stay with her. But my grandmother and my mom were at odds. They did not get along, and whatever the fight was between the two, Momma took this foolishness out on everyone she so-called loved.

I would help Big Momma out by setting the table for the three meals she provided to everyone. I would stand in amazement at how she would provide food with little or nothing much. It appeared that she had a donator, Mr. Willy. He owned a food truck, and what excess he had once he was done with his route, he would bring to her. I asked her one day how much he charged her for the excess food. She told me that the Lord was the provider. I wondered, too, how she felt that the Lord was the provider, yet she never attended church. At least that's what my momma said—attending church was the only way to get your needs met. You had to be present at church for the Lord to help you.

One rainy night, Mr. Willy stopped by at his usual time. When he came in, he eyed me while helping Big Momma put away the food. "Hey, young lady, how old are you now?" he asked. "I remember when your momma had you. You've grown so nice and pretty."

The way he looked at me made me feel so uncomfortable. In a way, it made Big Momma feel uncomfortable too. She threw me a shrewd, piercing look, grabbed Mr. Willy by the hand, and guided him to one of the back rooms. It was not long before I heard noises from her room like the ones I would hear from my daddy when he made his visits to those women. Sometimes I had to hear it when Momma had company from those jokers I didn't like. Her squeaky bed made these loud crunching noises. I could not tell if it was the sound of the bed or the fact that they both made interesting noises that was so repugnant. Were they jumping on the bed, and if so, why?

Although it was raining the night that Mr. Willy visited Big Momma, I decided to sit on the front porch. I wasn't sure of what they were doing, but it nauseated me. What I did learn, however, was the results that they all got from making those noises. Without working multiple jobs, Daddy always had money in his pocket. Big Momma was never hungry, and she could help others. Momma, well, she had a roof and a nice ride.

I decided to move back home with Momma after one of Big Momma's tenants and Mr. Willy said some grown-up stuff to me. Big Momma got mad about it, but for some reason, she was angrier with me—as if I'd said horrible things to them. She told me that I needed to take my "fast self" back to Momma and allow her to take care of me because I was causing problems in her house. I called Momma to tell her I needed to come home. She held the phone for a long time, and then she said, "Aight," and hung up.

The school year had started. In a way, I was looking forward to going back. This past summer was only me being tossed back and forth from one home to another. In homeroom, I noticed a new guy, and he was cute. I took a seat next to him because I was tired of hanging around the knuckleheads from years past.

The new guy kept looking at me, and I looked at him too. I tried to dress differently this year by stealing clothes from my momma's closet. What little money my daddy would give me, Momma would take some, stating that she needed the money for food because I ate too much. I didn't understand why she would say that. I mean, I was her daughter, for Christ's sake. I thought that most parents would do anything to take care of their own. Not my momma, though. She only looked out for herself.

My birthday was coming up, and I was eager to turn sixteen. This meant driving and, hopefully, a car. All these thoughts were flashing back and forth while newbie was trying to get my attention. I had a moment of total embarrassment.

"Hey, what is your name?" he asked. "My name is Mario. Mario Whitfield."

I jotted his name down in my tablet. Not sure why, but I did. "Mario, my name is Nicole. So are you new here?"

The teacher shushed me.

Embarrassed again. Of course he is new. Why did I ask that dumb question? Mario laughed and then entered his phone number in my phone. This time, I blushed. I think for my sixteenth birthday, I'm going to have a boyfriend, I told myself. I couldn't wait to share my space with someone whom, perhaps, I could make noises with—you know, he was a guy and I was a girl. I figured it must be something between the two.

After school, I stopped by my daddy's house. As usual, he had company. I did not have any intention of staying long, just long enough to get some money so I could up my wardrobe for my junior year in school. I did not want to dress like a little girl anymore. It was time to change and to grow up.

My daddy opened the door and greeted me with a warm hug. I peered past him and saw a woman I recognized from my neighborhood. When we made eye contact, I made sure that I took a good look at her. To distract me, Daddy reached into his pocket and pulled out a wad of money, leading me into the kitchen. "Baby girl, how was your first day of school? I am proud of you. You only have one more year remaining for school." The words "one more year" resonated in my head. This was Momma's new mantra. She would say this with joy and follow up with the statement that after graduation, I had to move out. Before I could reply to my daddy, the mystery lady had come into the kitchen and was eyeballing the money in my hand. Maybe she had just given him the money; she sure did not like that I had it in my hands. To comfort everybody, I quickly put it in my purse. "Daddy, school seems like it's going to be good this year. No problem as an honor student either."

The woman peered at me again and cleared her throat. For some reason, Daddy did not look her way. So she got caught in her feelings and walked away.

"Daddy, am I interrupting something? I mean…"

My daddy brought me close to him. "Naw, naw. You're good. In fact, she was just about to leave. Are you hungry?"

I looked in the living room to see if this woman was about to leave, and it did not appear to me that she was. "Daddy, I think I should leave. Thanks for the money." I got on my toes to give him a big hug. "I love you, Daddy."

For some reason, he hugged me as tight as he could. "I love you too, baby girl. Be careful on your way home, OK?"

I walked out and looked at the woman's car. She drove a white Jaguar. Just like the one—"Oh shucks!" I said aloud. "She's the owner of the rental house we live in. This is awful!" Some people have no integrity, I thought. I knew that she knew who I was besides being my daddy's daughter.

On the way home, I felt irritated. I started to feel as though I needed to become resistant to all the people who said that they loved me. If I could just get through the school year and go away for college, I'd be OK, I thought. There's nothing here anymore to keep me here.

I did not want to be a part of passing down bad omens with my momma, Big Momma, and now, the first man in my life, Daddy.

I took out my phone and dialed Mario. The phone rang half a ring, and he immediately picked up. "Hello, Nicole. What took you so long to call me?"

We both started laughing, and we talked all the way home and kept talking until midnight. I now had a new confidant and friend.

My relationship with Mario grew fast. We were so compatible. In fact, I no longer was home much. I started to spend time at his house. His mom was nice, and she worked at night. Mario and I would study together, watch movies, and have dinner. His mom kept her refrigerator stocked with all sorts of goodies. I learned how to cook at his place, because Momma often had company while she reminded me how many months, days, hours, and seconds I had left in her rented home—the home of the woman whom my daddy could give two cares about. Yeah, I could've said something to Momma. But the days were becoming increasingly competitive between me and her men friends. I rarely had the opportunity to talk to her. I was constantly interrupted by one of her friends or lover. She'd often say that I wanted attention, when she noticed one of her men friends staring at me. Basically, I figured it out that she wanted me gone so that she could scream or make the bed squeak as much as she wanted.

I finally figured out the part with the bed noises too. I asked Mario what on earth that was all about, and he offered to explain it to me. My curiosity caused me to lose my virginity to Mario. Why didn't he just choose to *tell* me? I felt that he had become like all the others, acting for their own selves and not to protect me. I learned what the bed noises were about, but it still did not make sense to me why two people would make those sounds like I often heard from Big Momma, Mr. Willy, Momma, and those dreadful women Daddy fooled around with. And I wondered if I, too, could benefit just as they did.

After graduation, Momma stuck by her word. There were no big congratulations for me; instead, there was an eviction. She packed my things and told me, "Good luck, and try not to get pregnant." How could someone warn her supposed daughter about pregnancy when she'd never taught me about my periods, sex, or life? There was no grace period or anything on moving out.

I moved in with my daddy for a while. The women were so jealous of me that there were times when I would have to leave. These women were my dad's paychecks. So to keep them happy and put a roof over my head, I had to find a place to go. Eventually, I just continued to bounce between Big Momma's house and my momma's house.

Mario and I had kind of fallen off. Mario was accepted at New York University, and he left. During school breaks, we saw each other less and less. His momma said to me one day, "Now, Nicole, you need to find your own. I let your little fast butt crash here sometimes, but you're not about to ruin my son's life with a baby or taking care of a family. It's time for you to get your own."

I was so hurt by those words. That was the one place where I could lay my head. And I knew that she knew that I was there at her place.

I quickly grew to resent my family. I found myself hanging at coffee shops, libraries, and the mall just to kill time. While journaling one day, I overheard a conversation between some people about reinvention. That word sound so good to my ears and my heart. Why not just leave the past behind by erasing my past and becoming someone else? What would be my strategy? I didn't have a job. I decided not to attend postsecondary school. I was now considered an adult, and I had to make some big-time adult decisions. My reinvention would be an entirely new me.

Several guys were in and out of my life after Mario. I was looking for Mr. Goodbar. I had sex with these guys in search of the things that I saw and heard from my family. What made them react to things the way they did? I wondered. What was this deal with bed squeaking and the noise making? There was still nothing—no noise for me or money. No one offered stability. Just "I will call you later," and they never would call again.

One afternoon, I met this dude named Rico at the coffee shop. I watched him enter the store, observed how he placed his order for a coffee. He sat at a table across from me. I pretended to be busy surfing the Internet. He came and sat at the table next to me and started a conversation about using the electrical outlet for his devices. I nodded and gave back a soft smile. His nails were nicely manicured, and his cologne was that of sweetness. He introduced himself as a real estate broker and revealed that he was five years older than I was. We talked and laughed, and I decided that I should leave before it got dark.

He noticed that I'd said little about myself, but I did express an interest in a job. He gave me his card, and I promised I would meet him in the same spot the next day. As I walked off, Rico shouted, "Hey, Ms. Lady, you did not tell me your name."

I thought, No, I did not. "I'll tell you tomorrow," I said.

Rico shook his head and took a sip of his coffee. "OK, beautiful. Tomorrow, it is."

I walked out feeling my worst and my best at the same time. My best because he acknowledged me; my worst because, really, who was I and what did I have going for me?

I unlocked the front door to my daddy's house. The woman who drove the white Jaguar, well, I guess that it wasn't her day. As I went in, the house was in complete darkness. I went to my room and locked the door behind me. I took the card that Rico had given me and decided to look up this well-spoken man.

Several images of him appeared along with entries regarding his business ventures. I can't talk to this man, I thought. I don't have shit to offer.

Suddenly, flashes of my family members and me began to cross my mind—I felt I could readily identify everything that they represented and the invaluable lessons that were either taught or demonstrated.

The next day, I met Rico. I was still playing games by not giving up my name. I think he must have liked it because he went along with it. The beautiful thing was that I could take a risk with him. I had nothing to lose, for I didn't have anything. All my life, no one had seemed to feel that I was worth anything either.

We sipped on tea, coffee, you name it. Finally, we were about to be a couple. At that point in my life, I needed someone to care about and take care of me. Wasn't that the way it was done? Security. Stability. I felt as if I could let my guard down—well, some but not too much.

Rico learned that I was not employed and that my ride was the bus. He said, "No worries." He offered to take me home.

"Oh yeah, about home. Let me explain..."

Rico smiled at me. "You don't have to go there either. Come on. Are you ready to go?"

I returned his smile. I wasn't so sure of what was next, but whatever it was, it had to be far better than my current situation. I grabbed his hand and felt an inner peace.

"Hey, Rico. My name is Vee, Vee Jaye."

He stopped and turned toward me. "You f**king kidding me? If I didn't know any better, I'd say a name like that is short for *vagina*. I mean, you do realize this, right?"

My sentiments exactly. He said what my thoughts were. Yes, vagina. And guess what? This vagina is going to take care of me. That night, not only did I figure out what the bed noises were about, but I also learned how to sing, how to make up vowels and new words, you name it. Thinking back on my family, it was the vagina that got the rent paid, put food on the table, and put money in the pockets. I couldn't help who I had become. It was in the DNA. It was inbred.

Blotted

y last client ran over his paid time, as always. He complained about both of his parents, having too much money, and where and how long the next family vacation should be. This type of client disgusted me. They didn't have any real problems, just complaints. They were over-privileged. In fact, there was no clinical name for such clients. Once they finished their sessions with me and I walked them out to the receptionist's desk, I had high hopes of their not returning.

I watched Mr. Cassidy in hopes of his waving good-bye. Instead, he turned around with a grin and an appointment card. As I returned to my office, I picked up my mother's picture, thinking about the many hard years she provided for me. Whatever I wanted to be professionally, she supported my ideas and dreams. I chose a career as a psychologist in order to give back. That was my duty. So many people in our community suffered from trauma and mental illness. Some illnesses were so severe that other family members didn't recognize them because they appeared to be the norm. I wanted to put a stop to that. Some illnesses were escalated due to trauma or life itself. Once the person was at his or her breaking point, it spread like a virus.

My mother was my everything. She never spoke harshly against my sperm-donor dad. I did not have a relationship with him. He decided to move on with his family, and I became a "bad decision." My mother said that he was someone who hung around in the area where she worked, and then I came along. No details. Too much pain for her. The only truth that I knew was that he'd made the decision not to be a dad to me. Did he even know I existed? Just how much information, if any, did my mother withhold? Whatever the case, we adjusted well in our lives. I completed college and graduated at the top of my class. To say that I didn't need him would be an understatement. All kids needed both parents. My mother was a female, and there were some things a woman couldn't teach a boy. Dad missed baseball games. He missed the honors program, all of it. I remembered looking up in the stands, imagining his waving at me, not knowing who he was or what he looked like. Awful? Maybe. Every now and then, it broke my heart. How could a man not be there for his kid, no matter the circumstances? The residue lingered. Therefore, I buried myself in my work.

I had no time for a relationship either. I tried, but I always found myself analyzing the female with this issue and that issue and missing out on what could have been a great thing. Who was I to think that we were flawless? For me to have become successful, I had to put my past to rest. But I needed to confront this me, this "residue," and meet this man…maybe.

There were times, too, when I struggled with my sexuality. I had a love for women, but never had I gotten close to any of them. I had too much anger wrapped up with visions of my mom's suffering—suffering to make ends meet and to raise me by herself. The flip side was hate and disgust. Men repulsed me. Why would my mom have any dealings with a married man? Not judging her, but this only complicated life.

My feelings for men would come and go. I figured because my father was not in my life, acceptance by any man would do. I had not physically been with a man. However, every now and then, I would fantasize about being with one. Either way, both ideas were repugnant. Something inside of me wanted to seek revenge—revenge toward a woman and revenge toward my father. As a psychologist, I had to deal with clients like that.

My next client was a medium-height, nicely built woman. On the outside, she appeared to be well put together; this was only because she wore designer from head to toe. I was not against flashing labels on things that were nice to wear and drive, but that shouldn't consume people. She set her bag on the floor and strutted over to the window. I was not sure if she came in to flirt or to get "fixed."

"So Ms.—"

"No, please," she interrupted. "No names today. Let's get to know each other. I'll start with you."

I chuckled. How dare this woman come into my office and take over? It kind of turned me on. "OK," I responded. "What would you like to know?"

The woman walked back toward me and sat on the chaise, crossing her legs slowly. "How long have you been in people's heads, Doctor? I mean, what made you choose this profession? Or did it choose you?"

I had to think about it for a minute before I responded. "I can say that it chose me. I've always wanted to help the community and give back to people so that they can be their healthiest. No matter how your physical report reads, if you're struggling or battling in the mind, physicality is void. Do you agree?"

The woman nodded. She then began to walk around my office, touching my diplomas, reading the plaques and awards that beamed from the bookshelf. She then sat on my desk.

With embarrassment, I glanced at my chart to read her brief introduction and check her picture to be sure that I wasn't being railroaded with some foolery. "Um, Ms.——"

Again, she shushed me with her index finger over my lips. This time, it angered me. Obviously, this woman had come into my office to play games.

I stood up and adjusted my jacket and necktie. "Look, I am going to ask you to not do that again. Furthermore, it would be best if we end this meeting."

The woman jumped down from my desk. "Look, I did not mean to disrespect you or get you all tied up in a bunch. This is my way of becoming familiar with others before letting my guard down."

I shook my head, thinking about what could possibly be going on in that crazy head of hers. "I understand that. However, it is unprofessional to sit on a desk and avoid the purpose for which you're here in the first place, right? I mean, to make progress and——"

Lo and behold, she interrupted me again. This time, with a phone call. I thought, No, she's not going to answer the phone. But just like that, she did. I kindly moved toward her and escorted this inconsiderate, rude woman from my office. She could get assistance elsewhere. I was relieved when she left.

As soon as I returned to my office, I heard the voice which was the sound of a beautiful woman speaking with my administrative assistant, Kasha. I turned around to listen to determine if she was a client. It turned out that she was a friend of my assistant.

"Doc, I am about to take off early, if that's OK with you," Kasha said. "Your afternoon is clear, unless…"

As I turned around before walking back into my office, I extended my hand to shake the hand of that breath of fresh air. "Hi," I said. "And you are?"

The woman blushed and looked at her friend. "My name is Shana and…"

My assistant looked at me warily. "His name is doctor. Come on, girl, we have to go!"

I cleared my throat and responded to Kasha. "Yeah, yeah, we are done for the day. Enjoy the rest of your evening, Shana, and especially you, Kasha." The fact that Kasha had interrupted me and did not allow me to meet her lovely friend annoyed me. "I'll take care of you later, Ms. Kasha," I mumbled to myself. I could hear the bell of the elevator as I returned to my office.

As an employee, little did she know that I had complete control over everything that I did. I didn't trust anyone. No one. Last year, I presented Ms. Kasha with a tracker phone, which let me see her location and hear what she was doing all the time. I could not afford to have any fallout from her access to my office, my clients, or my life.

Sitting at my desk, I swiveled the chair back and forth, thinking about my introduction to Shana. This Shana woman intrigued me. There was something about her I could not resist thinking about. I was not sure why I even bothered, considering that I never made time for anyone anyway.

My phone buzzed. I glanced at it. It was someone calling from an unknown number. This made my heart race with anxiety. I reached into my drawer to take two pills. Even as a psychologist, I had days that I needed pharmaceutical assistance to maintain my calm. My phone rang again, and then the caller hung up. I threw my phone into the desk drawer and logged on to my tablet. As I adjusted the volume, I could clearly hear Kasha talking to Shana.

"Girl, why did you cut me off with the introduction from your boss? He's cute, and he's a doctor," Shana said.

"Yes, he is a doctor and very handsome. But each time I attempt to ask a personal question, he changes the subject. There's a picture of some woman on his desk. I take it that she's his mom. It's like he's a loner. I think he's a momma's boy," Kasha explained.

I thought, Momma's boy? That bitch!

"No other family, wife, girlfriend, or children. I just don't want you to get mixed up with him. You're doing really well now that you left that playboy Brendan alone," Kasha continued.

"Yes, moving away from Brendan was the best thing that I could do for *me*. He was never going to settle down. He, well,

I allowed him to string me along for five long years, and what did I get from it? Heartache," Shana said.

"Could you bring us another glass of Meiomi?" Kasha requested. Judging from that, I assumed they were in a restaurant, and she was talking to a waiter. Then she said, "What about this new guy from Chicago you met at the convention, Timothy Johnson, the investment banker?"

Shana was silent for a moment, and I imagined her sipping her wine. "He's a great guy. Actually, he's perfect. No kids. A home. But he lives in a different state. Besides, I am taking one day at a time."

I clicked on the locator to see where the two of them were dining. I quickly grabbed my keys and locked up the office. They had not gone far. I was there in less than fifteen minutes. As I sat in my car and watched them from across the street, I decided I would wait to go into the restaurant. Then I saw them settling the check. Perfect. I walked in gingerly and sat at the bar. As they got up from the table, I pretended to drop my fork on the floor. "Oh, excuse me. I am such a clumsy person. Oh, Kasha! What a pleasant surprise. You come here often?"

Kasha was very reluctant to answer. "Um, yes. What are you doing here, Doctor? I thought maybe you were at the office transcribing patient notes." Kasha seemed to be a little suspicious of my appearance at the restaurant.

"No, no. I got hungry and decided to grab a bite to eat. Where are you all headed?"

"We're——" Shana proceeded to say.

"We are headed home," Kasha interjected. "See you in the morning, Dr. Wallace."

I watched as they walked out and waited for the valet to bring their cars around. I pulled out my tablet to hear what Kasha had to say.

"You know, he gives me the creeps. I just feel something's really weird about him."

"Kasha, your radar is always up about everyone. You should be OK with him, right? After all, you do work for him," Shana said.

I could see Kasha waving as she entered her vehicle.

I was having some awful mood swings. Just the thought of Kasha controlling Shana—not allowing me to see her—was dramatic. This angered me, and I wanted to do something to hurt Kasha. Instead, I called Kasha and told her to cancel my appointments for the day. The urge to find out who my father was was tearing me to pieces. I took a drive by my mother's house. Maybe she had some concealed information on this man. I knew she wouldn't be home; it was her day to play tennis and have lunch with some friends. I carefully let myself into her townhome. "Let's see, Ms. Wallace, where do you keep my birth certificate and important papers?"

I went into her office and noticed a two-drawer filing cabinet. I started at the bottom and went through her things. Mom had all sorts of pictures stashed away. "Hmm, a picture of her during her pregnancy." Someone had to have taken that picture of her. I continued to go through the papers, and then I came across a paper folded nicely with *TJS—Illinois* printed on it. "Who is TJS?" I asked myself.

As I continued to look through the documents, I found letters from this TJS. "I wonder if this is my father? Let's read one of the letters, shall we?"

The letters were from my father, all right. The envelopes did not have any return addresses on them. Just the Illinois postmark. This man seemed to love my mother, but for the sake of a family, he made the choice to stay there. I flipped through more papers and read the final correspondence from him. He begged Mother to abort me or give me up for adoption. Aha! A picture! Damn, I thought. Looking at him, I could see why Mother couldn't deny him. The SOB was nice looking, based on this picture. It was an older picture, but based from his appearance, he had not transformed too much. Only by thirty-two years.

In the letter, he wrote that if she did not terminate the pregnancy or give me up for adoption, he would never have anything to do with me. He would deny my existence.

Just like that: deny, blot out. I was a disgrace.

I continued to go through her things and saw papers detailing Mother's admittance to a mental institution due to depression and thoughts of suicide. I got angry as I continued reading. There was more. More letters and info concerning my father. Once Mother got out of the mad house, she got into trouble for stalking and showing up at his home, scaring his wife.

I put all the papers back. I'd had enough of reading how my mother had fallen apart. Maybe he'd lied to her and she had not known that he was married. Perhaps it was too late, and she conceived me without knowing he had a family. I couldn't imagine Mother being naïve. Not my mother. In order for me to heal, I needed answers. I looked forward to the day when I'd have my own children, whether I adopted or figured out whom I wanted to be with. Now I was on the hunt for TJS. He and his family had no right to attempt to get rid of me. I must avenge my mother's name and the things she'd endured.

Shana

Never say never. Vowing I would not date long distance——that entire idea has been thrown out the window. Timothy has come to Atlanta for business and, of course, to catch up with me. Timothy is mature and the perfect gentleman. In fact, I really like him, more than I anticipated. We'll see. Men do it all the time. They have a main babe, and then there are the others. Besides, because he lives in Chicago, we talked and emailed a lot, which this gave us the opportunity to get to know each other much better.

It has been a long time since I have been romantic with someone. I definitely do not want to rush anything and make a mistake. And then there is Dr. Wallace. He is good-looking and intelligent. The beauty of him is that he is mysterious and intriguing. He always keeps me wondering and in suspense. I feel closer to him than to Timothy. Kasha always warns me about Dr. Wallace, tells me to be careful and all of that. We'll see. I can handle myself. But tonight, I have a date with Timothy, and who knows how far I may go?

Date Night

Timothy was right on time. It had been raining all day and night, so I decided to order in and have our date at my place. I watched as Timothy explored my artwork. I am an avid collector. I gracefully walked around with him, explaining the pieces one by one. We talked practically the entire night. We ate, drank, and danced. The rain finally stopped, and we went up to the rooftop to complete the night. For once in a long time, I felt good. Timothy was a cool person, and I was willing to take things a little bit further. What really topped off the night was that he FaceTimed his family so that we could be introduced informally. First, his mother came on. She was a beautiful woman. Mrs. Johnson had long gray-white hair that hung down her back. One would think that she was a Native American. Then Mr. Johnson came on. He appeared to be tall, sleek, and full of life. He and the missus were a perfect pair.

Timothy and I kissed and fooled around. Hell, it had been a long time for me, and girl had some wants right then. When Timothy was touching me, I did not have any thoughts of past hurts or fears. That was what I wanted, and being with Timothy then was so satisfying.

Timothy invited me to fly back to Chicago with him. I closed my office for a few weeks and planned accordingly. Before I left, I hit up my girlfriend Kasha. "Hey, K. How is it going?"

Kasha let out a long sigh. "Girl, where in the heck have you been, and why have I not heard from you? I was about to come over and look for you."

"I know, girl," I said. "I had every intention of contacting you. I guess I got caught up. Timothy came in for a few days, and now...Don't you judge me. I am on my way to Chicago to meet his family. Can you believe it?"

Kasha was quiet for a moment. "Girl, are you sure you're not moving too fast? I mean, well, considering the bad break with what's his name, it's too fast. Just be careful. How long are you gone for, girl? Send me addresses, aight?"

I started to smile. My girl Kasha understood. "Kasha, I am just enjoying myself, you know. All those years I wasted with Brendan. It's time to move forward. Hey, look, it's almost time for me to board. I'll text you the information. Hey, thanks, and I love you. I gotta go! Bye, girl."

I sent Kasha the text: *I am flying into O'Hare on Delta. His parents' home address is 70010 West Ontario Lakes, and I am staying at the Hilton downtown.*

Dr. Wallace
I'm so disgusted, I thought. This heifer has been ignoring my calls, roses, cards, texts, you name it. Now I know why. Guess

I will have to pay her ass a visit with her new boyfriend. I don't appreciate being ignored. I reached into my desk drawer and swallowed a few pills as if they were mints. I've heard more than I can handle. I heard the whole thing. My girl…well, maybe she's not my girl, but she likes me, and she knows how I feel about her. My girl, Shana, is acting like a slut-breathing whore. She's off to the house of some man she doesn't know anything about. Women! They can be so vulnerable. I've been the perfect gentleman with her. Taking things slow. I guess I was too slow.

"Kasha," I called, "please cancel my afternoon appointments."

Kasha ran into my office. "But Dr. Wallace, you've broken the appointment with Mr. Cassidy several times and—"

I hit my desk. "Kasha, please cancel my appointment. Just contact my colleague Dr. Glenn. He can see Mr. Cassidy instead."

Kasha looked at me all strange. "Sir, is everything OK? I mean, you look flushed. Are you coming down with something? I can—"

I was so frustrated with Kasha. She never followed directions. "Kasha, no. I am leaving for the day. Lock up, and I will call later to provide you with updates. OK?"

I locked my drawer and the door to my office and left. I was desperate to go after Shana. Why would she do me like this? And why was she a whore? I needed to save her. She was acting out because of this Brendan guy who'd hurt her. Timothy. I got on the highway to head to Hartsfield Airport. Once I arrived in Chicago, someone would have to go. I would bring Ms. Shana back with me. Of course, she'd probably be unwilling at first, but I had something for that.

Shana

We arrived at the home of Timothy's parents, and it was just as I expected. As the gates opened, I saw the letter *J* worked into the design of the metalwork. We drove up the winding drive-way and were met by Mr. and Mrs. Johnson.

As I waited to get out of the car, I inhaled deeply, taking it all in. Timothy came over to open my door and quickly introduced me to his parents. Mrs. Johnson grabbed me by the hands and walked me into their home.

I thought *I* had an art collection. But the Johnsons had paintings and sculptures in every room. My phone kept vibrating, and I took a moment to glance at it. It was Kasha. I wondered why she was calling me. I will call her back later, I thought.

Mr. Johnson walked toward me. "My, young lady, you are just as beautiful in person as you are on that measly phone. For my son to bring someone home, you must be someone pretty special!"

I wiped my sweaty palms on my jeans. "Thank you so much, Mr. Johnson. Your hospitality is more than generous. You and Mrs. Johnson have a beautiful home. I love the paintings."

The Johnsons have class and style, I thought. It seems like this time, I picked the right guy. Loving parents and a couple.

One heck of a son who's fine as hell and great in bed. And he has me in his parents' home. A girl couldn't ask for more.

Kasha

"Damn, damn! Shana, pick up!" I knew all along that Dr. Wallace was weirded out. When he continued to cancel his clients' appointments, I figured he was going through some sort of change.

He just flew out so fast that he thought he'd locked the door to his office, but he hadn't. He did not shut down his computer either. This mofo was on his way to Chicago to stalk my girl.

"C'mon Shana! Pick up the damn phone already!"

Dr. Wallace

I checked into my hotel room to come up with a plan to get to Shana. Somehow, I needed to convince her that this guy was wrong for her. I swallowed more pills as I flicked my pencil back and forth. I knew if I would just intentionally show up, it would freak her out. She did not appear to be the type who took surprises well. I decided to lie low. Besides, she was staying at the Hilton, which was not far from me at the Embassy Suites.

I was sure they would catch dinner or something. But first, I needed to make a stop at a department store and purchase a gift set of knives. Then I'd be on my way.

Shana

I checked my phone and noticed that Kasha and Dr. Wallace had called me several times. I hope everything is OK, I thought. I'll send a text: *Hi there! I hope everything is fine with you. I am out of town right now visiting some friends. I will get back to you once I am home. Talk to you soon.*

"There!" I said to myself. "Now let me call Ms. Kasha."

Timothy came up from behind and put his arms around me. "Hey, beautiful. What are you out here doing? Miss me?"

I quickly put away my phone. "Hey, you. I'm just admiring this beautiful property your parents own. They've done an excellent job with the landscaping."

"Yeah, Mom has a lot to do with the lawn and plantings. Sometimes she gets out here to work in the garden with the gardener. She says that working in the yard helps her to stay young and vibrant."

"Yes, she is a beautiful woman. Nice, too, to allow me to come into her home."

Timothy kissed me on the forehead. "Anything for you. I knew when I first met you that you're the one for me. I don't want to waste years dating and losing time with space between us. Sometimes when folk date forever, it allows that space for arguing and fighting, and therefore, there's a change of heart and mind."

Mrs. Johnson came out to the front porch. "Timothy and Shana, I hope you all don't mind. It's not often my son comes home and has dinner with us, so I've invited a few of our relatives. It will be just like old times."

"Mom, you don't have to go out of your way for me," Timothy said. "This also puts Shana in the spotlight, which, I am sure, has given her a true sense of nervousness." He turned to me and said, "But, Shana, I will protect you from anything crazy. My family can be a little bit nuts."

We all laughed. Mrs. Johnson grabbed my hand. "Shana, dear, please walk with me to unlock the gate, so that the guest could walk by foot from the main entrance. This way we don't have to worry about allowing the guests in and out. This will give us an opportunity to do some chatting."

I glanced at Timothy and put my shades on. "Sure thing, Mrs. Johnson."

I gave Timothy a kiss before leaving. I felt like a million dollars being at their home.

Dr. Wallace

I decided to take an Uber to the Johnsons' house. I did not care anymore. I did not like the fact that Shana had further insulted my love for her by sending an insensitive text. She could've very well stepped away to phone me.

I am going to make her pay, I thought. Just my showing up would be shock enough for her. But most important, I need to eradicate Timothy. Lure him away and get rid of him so that Shana and I can be together once and for all. This way, I can continue to make Mother happy. It will make Mother so happy if I have a son, a wife—a complete family—because she could not have that. After I take care of Timothy, I will locate this TJS to avenge my mother.

When we approached the Johnson residence, I asked the driver to let me out at the bottom of the driveway. "Hmm, they have company," I said to myself. "Well, guess who else is coming to dinner?"

Kasha

I am going to try to reach Shana one more time, I thought. Please, Lord, have her answer the ph—"Shana, thank goodness you picked up!"

"Yeah, hey," she said. "We are about to have dinner. What's going on?" Then she tucked the phone against her shoulder and said, "Yes, Timothy, I will be right there. I am on the phone with Kasha." Turning back to me, she said, "Talk fast. I have to go."

I took a few deep breaths. "Shana, Dr. Wallace is in Chicago. I think he may be stalking you."

Shana laughed. "Stalking me? The only person who pulled that stunt was that dang Brendan. Why do you say that? Hello?

Hello? Kasha, my phone is about to die. Let me ring you back. Hello? Hello?"

Dr. Wallace

Boldly and in awe, I blended in with the caterers as I walked through the corridors of the Johnsons' beautiful home. There were paintings everywhere. I could hear the laughter of the guests. I just wanted to get close to Timothy and then make a run for it. I'd decided to deal with Shana later. I wanted it to look like a robbery. I would badly injure him and then be gone.

An older man walked into the living room. I guessed he was Timothy. The man approached me and asked, "Excuse me. Can I help you with something? Timothy, is he one of your friends?"

I bit my lip. I could not believe it. The old man standing before me was my father. TJS—Timothy Johnson Sr. I pulled out the knife and lunged for Timothy Jr. The knife cut him right in the neck.

The old man stumbled toward a drawer and pulled out a gun. I whipped the knife, cutting the son's neck again so that he would bleed to death. At this point, I no longer cared what would happen, but I needed to let the old man know who the hell I was.

"Hey, you don't know me, do you?" I said.

The old man yelled to people in the other room to call 911. He bent over to stop the bleeding from his son's neck. I started poking the knife at him, trying to get him to react. "I am your son, you old bastard! Yes, what are the odds? And that tramp Shana led me here. She knew all about this."

Shana hurried into the room. "What's going on? Wallace, what are you doing?"

Mr. Johnson turned to face Shana. I took the knife and wheeled at the old man, stabbing him in the heart. As he crumpled, a gun went off. Suddenly, I felt my head hit the floor. I could hear screams. The knife dropped to the floor. Suddenly, everything began to fade.

A week later, Mrs. Johnson placed flowers on her husband's and son's graves—a red rose for the former and a white rose for the latter. I stood back in disbelief at all that had transpired. Mrs. Johnson grabbed my hand, and we walked back to the car. I felt so bad for her. What would she do next? How could she go on? I decided to say something.

"Mrs. Johnson, I can stay if you like. My friend Kasha can check on my gallery to make sure things are OK."

Mrs. Johnson removed her hat and her gloves. "No, baby, I am just fine. For years, I asked Timothy Sr. about that child, yet he denied him. Erased him. Blotted him out. I guess what goes around comes around. All these years, he thought Timothy Jr. was his, but he wasn't." Mrs. Johnson started laughing. "Now we all can finally rest."

~Fall~

As the leaves change in the fall, so should we.

~L. A. Davis

Today, You Don't Get to Choose

*E*veryone tended to think that I was spoiled and that I got my way. Maybe this was true. I never caused any issues with my parents. For my last year in high school, I decided to move in with Dad. The divorce was hard on me. Momma would say that I favored him, which I did. Wasn't that what most girls do? My brothers, of course, were there to take care of Mom. Someone needed to take care of Dad.

Before school started, Daddy figured I should have my own car, because I no longer lived with Mother and Daddy can afford to buy me a car. The first thing was learning how to drive. This should be an experience, I thought.

To my surprise, I learned quickly. Daddy was so patient. Once I got my license, we were off to the car lot. I was not too choosy. However, Daddy wanted me to drive the best. "I never want you to be stranded anywhere," Daddy said.

I test-drove a new convertible BMW 325-white with tan seats. We also applied for a custom tag: "DADGIRL." My daddy doing this I caused me to be envied. But I did not care. My daddy loved me.

Some weekends, I would stop by to see Mom and my brothers. My oldest brother, Andrew, decided to enlist in the air force. The twins, Marcus and Marion, stayed home to attend community college and work.

"Girl, where did you get that car? I mean, did Albert get that for you?" Momma screamed.

"Yes, he did. I had nothing to do with it."

Momma mumbled under her breath, "He never done anything for your brothers." She walked around the car and then sat in the front seat. "It's a bit small, don't you think?"

I shook my head. Why couldn't she just be happy for me? If anything was related to Daddy, it was a problem. "No, Momma, I don't think that it's small. It is just right for me."

She turned up her lips. "Albert can afford both the insurance and the note? Hmm. Don't come to me asking for one red cent, Marcy. This is between you and your bourgie dad. If it was up to me, you would have your little butt on that school bus. Ain't no high schooler or child of mine is deserving of such—unless you work for yourself."

By this time, my brother Marcus had come closer. He could tell I was in my feelings, so he put his arms around me to calm me down. A tear streamed down my cheek because I knew these feelings were all geared toward my dad and me being the only girl. My original plan was to stay and hang out, but after all of that, I thought it was best to leave. I hugged Marcus, put on my shades, and got into the car. That Saturday, my momma killed my happy and implanted how I should feel about my worth.

Once I got home, I pulled my car into the garage. I'd decided not to go joy riding. I sat in my room and played on social media. Daddy came in, shocked that I was there.

"Baby girl, why aren't you out with the top down, enjoying this special day?"

I hesitated to answer because I didn't want him to know that my sulky attitude was due to a woman gone mad. I turned to face Daddy. "Well, I stopped by Momma's house to see her and my broth—"

Daddy interrupted. "Sweetheart, don't tell me that your momma gave you a hard time about that car. Is that also the reason why you pulled into the garage?"

I nodded, feeling that I really didn't deserve what Daddy had done for me.

"Baby girl, don't worry about your mother. I don't know what's wrong with that woman. You see, that's why your brother Andrew got the hell on. It seems like the older she gets, the more of a shrew she's becoming. Whatever I can do for mine, I will. And I got a feeling, too, that she mentioned that I didn't do anything for your brothers, huh? Let me tell you something. Your momma just wanted everything to be about her and no one else."

I started crying. I did not want my daddy to revisit any of the pain that Momma had caused him in the past.

"Why don't you go out and have some fun, baby girl. Go enjoy that nice ride and be careful."

I ended up driving out and hanging with some friends from school. If Daddy knew that I was hanging with one of the

Mitchell brothers, he would have a fit. They were notorious for being "bad boys," and their family was out of control.

Dwayne had dropped out of school but never caused anyone any problems. He tried to talk to me years ago, but my parents and brothers weren't having it.

That night, though, I decided to hang out with them for once. Dwayne had a sister named Teresa. She was cool, but I did not feel that she wanted me around. She had a problem with my being with her brother. Every time he gave me a compliment, she would roll her eyes or say something crazy to him.

It wasn't long before I stopped visiting my mother. I got tired of her negative remarks. As long as Daddy did for me, she did not like it.

Eventually, my brothers left too. They would stop by only on holidays. All of us became distant, when at one time, we'd been close. Daddy and I were at odds too. He did not like Dwayne, but I loved him. My grades dropped because I was no longer focused on school, and eventually, I had to drop out and attend open campus. I was rebelling.

Momma said that Daddy gave me too much, whereas Daddy said that Momma didn't give me enough. I argued with them both and avoided them at all costs.

One evening, I came home, tipsy. Daddy met me at the door. "Give me your keys, baby girl!"

I looked at him as if he'd told me to get out of his house. "Why?" I said. "You know I need this car to get back and forth to school."

Daddy blocked me from going to my room and slamming the door as I always did. "I am going to ask you one last time," he said. "Give me those keys right now!"

I threw the keys at him, went to my room, packed some clothes, and left. What did I do wrong? I always came home, I thought. I know I messed up, but this time, Daddy went too far.

Dwayne told me I could stay at his place as long as I liked. I enjoyed waking up every day to Dwayne. I felt big because he was a bad dude, which meant that no one would ever step to me. My brothers got wind that I had left Daddy, and boy, were they angry! I did not care. I was grown, and I did not need them. Besides, Momma and Daddy should've thought about things when we were younger. If they had, we would not have been in this situation.

I missed my daddy, though. I heard that he wasn't doing too well. My aunt reached out to me, asking me to stop by and say hi to him. I immediately became defensive. How could I stop by anywhere? He took my freaking car for God's sake!

Everybody just kept telling me what I needed to do, but they weren't doing anything themselves. One day, Daddy called me to say that he was no longer going to pay my cell phone bill. We got into the biggest fight. "Daddy, how can you do this?" I said. "First, you took my car. Now the phone? What is the problem, Daddy?"

He paused for a moment. Then he said, "Why don't you let those people you hang with pay your phone bill? I am done."

Dwayne overheard my daddy speaking to me about the phone, and he took the phone from me. "Look, I will take care of it," he said to Daddy. "Do what you gotta do. You heard me."

I was shocked he spoke to my daddy that way. I did not want Dwayne to do that. I tried to dial Daddy back, but I could not get service. "Wow, I guess he wasn't playing. He really disconnected the phone."

For the next few days, I was miserable. I did not want to be at the Mitchells' home. Too many people in and out. I had no money. No fly clothes. No car. Nothing. Dwayne had started leaving me at home a lot as well. His sister would rub in my face that Dwayne had another girlfriend. I would never show my weakness to her. She was a hater. Oh wait, I no longer had anything. There was no reason for her to hate me. This had to be the worst.

One night, Dwayne came home smelling like the worst weed ever. One of his friends came into his room and started making passes at me. "Dwayne, aren't you going to check your boy?" I said. "Didn't you just hear him?"

Dwayne looked at me and snarled, "For what? You ain't my lady anymore. Look at you. You don't do shit. You ain't got nothing. Even your own daddy don't want you."

I was filled with rage when Dwayne said such true but vile things. I jumped up from the bed, grabbed what things I had, and left. I walked to the nearest corner store and waited for someone who was familiar to me to come in so I could ask if I could use her phone. I tried dialing my momma first. No answer. Next, I called one of my brothers. No answer.

"Girl, you know people don't answer to numbers they don't recognize," Patrice said. "Who you tryna call anyways?"

I sucked my teeth. "Somebody in my family so that they can come and get me. I left my bae, and I am tired and hungry."

Patrice said, "Look, you can crash at my spot tonight. Only for the night, though. My ol' man will be back tomorrow. He drives trucks."

I grabbed my backpack and headed down the street with Patrice. Her house reeked of dirty diapers, and it was dark and damp. She flipped the light switch, and three or four bugs rushed to the corner. I looked at her, and she stared back at me.

"Look, it ain't all fancy, but it's home," she said. Then she threw me a blanket that was full of lint and holes to cover up with. That night, I wept so hard, and I wanted to go home. Any home. What I would do if Daddy would forgive me. I prayed that the night would go as quick as possible. I would head his way, no matter how I had to get there. Just let daylight come quick.

The next day, I got up as if I had a job to go to. Patrice was already gone. She left a note telling me to turn the lock at the bottom to secure the door. I thought, Why even lock the door? There's no furniture or anything worth stealing.

I locked the bottom lock just as she asked and headed down the street. I was able to scrape up enough change to catch the train, and I walked the rest of the way to Daddy's house.

It was sweltering. The hottest day ever. As I got closer to the house, I noticed all sorts of cars parked near it. Maybe the neighbors are having a party or something, I thought. I got nearer and saw my mother on the front porch with her head down. She looked up and grabbed me. I was confused. Why was she there? And why were all those people there? I went inside and saw my aunts, Granny, and other family members. In Daddy's bedroom, my brothers were huddled together crying. My oldest brother, Andrew, wiped his face and grabbed me. "Baby girl, Daddy is gone."

Gone where? I thought. What is he talking about? I just talked to Daddy the other day. No, I yelled at him the other day. He didn't say anything to me then about leaving.

Andrew continued to try to make me understand. "The funeral home just came and took him. He had a heart attack. The doctor said that it was stress that killed him because he never had any heart problems before."

I sank to the floor. What had I done? How was it that I was the apple of his eye one minute—he'd stop his life for me and give me whatever I wanted—and then he just died?

Friday

The home-going service was so sad. I had no words to say because my last words had been horrible. I'd even allowed Dwayne to disrespect him. I did not say I was sorry. I would never have another chance to tell him I loved him. There would be no more times for Daddy to tell me how pretty and smart I was. All he wanted was the best for me and then some, but I didn't want those things for myself. I felt as if any minute, I would wake up just as I woke up at Patrice's house. Morning came, and I was able to get to Daddy's house. Maybe if I hadn't stopped at Patrice's house that night. Maybe, instead of looking for a phone, I should've caught that train ride. He would be here, and I would be with him. One last time, I wish I could have said, "Daddy, forgive me. I love you."

Stay in Your Lane

*Stay in your lane, sistah girl. For real, don't be
mad at me. Rejoice with me, for I am good in the
skin that I am in.*

*Stay in your lane, girl, please. Don't look at my
confidence or self-esteem as arrogance. Don't judge
my praise of my family or my worth as conceit or
boasting. Girl, rejoice with me.*

*Stay in your lane, ol' girl, 'cause out of
this—a past life of hurts, pains, and blundered
generational curses—caused my head to be held up
high and only a strut that the brothas like or for
you and others to admire.*

*Stay in your lane, sistah, when I don't do as you
do or how you think it should be done. Please don't
think, "She always must do things her way," but
rejoice that in my own, on my own, I express my
individuality and self-worth.*

*Stay in your lane, sistah girl, 'cause you come to
me with your issue, and I give you my opinion.
Don't suck your teeth with disregard, 'cause I've
heard and played the same role before. Instead,
rejoice with me because my story and your story
together can bring a sisterhood and a bond.*

*Stay in your lane. Oh, I didn't know that you think
that I think that I am all that, but rejoice, because
my Father says that I am the apple of His eye, and
so I can't help but be something awesome, unique,
and great.*

*Stay in your lane, sistah girl. I don't just do "me"
out of this; I try to do for others with love and
compassion, and I can be a helluva friend.*

*I told you, girl, to stay in your lane, because when
I enter a room, I bring in something that maybe
you want and think that you may need.*

*Yeah, I make mistakes. And flaws? Yes. Me perfect?
Nah, not me.*

*I'll rejoice and be glad anyway. I rejoice 'cause I
am good in the skin I am in. Why?*

Because I stay in my lane.

Acknowledgments

As I type these last pages, I always thank my Heavenly Father for everything, every journey, every season. You have blessed me, saved me, and given me many mercies and much grace. I am grateful.

To my hubby, Anthony, thank you for your patience and for being my biggest fan. To my beautiful children, Brea and Brandon, thank you for loving your mommy tirelessly. To my family—mothers Pat, Lottie, and Momma Byrd; mom-in-law, Annie; and sisters Kim and Tammy—thank you for your encouraging words.

Thanks to the "Think Tankers" book club members—Jacquel, Natalie, Renz, Rita, Saint, Selena, Susan, Traci, and Vernida—for encouraging me to write a book. Thanks to my sistahs Roshonda, Doreatha, Keecia, and Ronnie, who believed in me more than I believed in myself. I am grateful to my faithful readers and commentators Yadira, Kerri, Lenetra, Stephanie, Anissa, Shanna, Tauheeda, Bonnie, Cindy, Ella, Tunji, Jessica, Brenda, Bill, and Yunhwa, and to my hairdresser (any time I needed makeup or whatever), Risha Clark. I also thank my sistah and photographer, Gwen Johnson.

Finally, to any of you who read my material on my website, Facebook pages, and these pages, thank you for your support. Much love and blessings to you all.

L. A. Davis
E-mail: ladavisthscrivener@gmail.com
Website: www.ladaviswrites.com